The Frayed Ribbon

The Frayed Ribbon

R.W. HART

THE FRAYED RIBBON

iUniverse books may be ordered through booksellers or by contacting:

iUniverse
1663 Liberty Drive
Bloomington, IN 47403
www.iuniverse.com
1-800-Authors (1-800-288-4677)

Because of the dynamic nature of the Internet, any web addresses or links contained in this book may have changed since publication and may no longer be valid. The views expressed in this work are solely those of the author and do not necessarily reflect the views of the publisher, and the publisher hereby disclaims any responsibility for them.

Any people depicted in stock imagery provided by Thinkstock are models, and such images are being used for illustrative purposes only. Certain stock imagery © Thinkstock.

ISBN: 978-1-4917-8429-7 (sc)
ISBN: 978-1-4917-8430-3 (e)

Library of Congress Control Number: 2015959381

Print information available on the last page.

iUniverse rev. date: 12/10/2015

Sixteen Years Earlier

Gail Rollins had been prescribed bed rest for a high-risk pregnancy. To ensure compliance, she had been admitted to the hospital. Every sleepless night since being admitted, she had spent sitting on a chair looking out into the uneventful night. Tonight the scene outside her window was anything but uneventful. Flashing lights, reminiscent of a lighthouse beacon warning unsuspecting mariners of impending danger, broke through the darkness. Red and amber lights illuminated the swirling snow outside her hospital window as a weary Gail watched snowplows clear and sand the roads. Freezing rains followed by heavy snowfall had caught everyone unprepared. The early-morning commute resembled a dangerous game of bumper cars.

She watched the traffic a few minutes longer before standing from the uncomfortable hospital chair. Gail returned to her bed in an attempt to find a few more precious minutes of sleep. Just as her eyes closed, she heard the sound, by now all too familiar, of cars hitting cars on the street below. Part of her wanted to see how bad the multicar pileup was, but the other part just wanted sleep to come. She checked the time and sighed. It was almost time for the first visit from her nurse.

When Gail next opened her eyes, to the sound of the nurse entering the room, she noted that she had slept almost an hour before Kerri Fox arrived to record the blood pressure and pulse readings for her and the heart rates for the unborn twins. Kerri's free-flowing auburn hair suited her personality because she was always upbeat and cheerful, as if she had no worldly cares.

"Good morning, Gail. How are you today?" Kerri asked.

Gail stretched and gave a big yawn. "Aside from not sleeping again last night, I'm doing fine."

"I'll make that note in your chart for the doctor. Now let's see how mother and babies are doing today." Kerri went about her business.

As the final chart entry was made, Gail asked, "Did you see the accident on your way to work this morning?"

Kerri took a few moments to respond as she checked the IV bag and injected some medication into the line. "Which accident are you referring to?"

Gail motioned toward the window. "The accident just outside the hospital."

Kerri glanced toward the window. "No, I never saw that one. I came in the back way to avoid traffic."

Gail became curious as to how bad things were in the outside world. "How many accidents have there been?"

Kerri sighed. "There have been more than enough."

Gail sensed that something was bothering Kerri. By this time they should have been deep into a good conversation.

Kerri finished what she was doing and then checked the water jug on Gail's table. "So far this morning, there have been over a hundred reported accidents." Kerri paused. "A lot of them have caused serious injuries."

"That's not good."

"No, it isn't. The emergency rooms and the operating rooms in all the hospitals are already at capacity, and there are still many more injured people being transported by ambulance."

Her time in the hospital had helped Gail to sense what was happening by the actions of her caregivers, and Kerri was easy to read. Gail watched the subtle side-to-side motion of Kerri's head accompanied by a deep breath and a slow exhale. Kerri always exhibited these behaviors when the results of the readings were cause for concern, like this morning's readings must have been. After a few seconds, with the emotion of what she was feeling present in her normally controlled voice, Kerri said, "It's as if everyone forgot how to drive in these conditions."

It was apparent to Gail that Kerri had more to say when the sound of approaching sirens ended the conversation. Kerri went silent and left the room.

Gail's doctor came by later that morning, and she was unsettled when he studied her chart more intently than he had ever done before. She watched the doctor bite his lower lip and tap the corner of her chart with his pen as he read. Gail became concerned with this behavior and wondered if her condition had taken a turn for the worse. She gently rubbed her tummy and felt a baby kick as she waited nervously for her doctor to speak. When she was no longer able to handle the suspense, she asked, "Is there a problem?"

It was evident that her question had surprised the doctor. The tone of his voice and his mannerisms seemed different from other days, and he fumbled with the chart as he placed it in the holder. "Everything is great."

Gail breathed a sigh of relief. "That's good to hear."

"Yes. In fact, your condition has improved enough that I might send you home today."

Normally, if the doctor had told her that she could go home, Gail would have been dressed and at the door. But today something felt off. Kerri's actions when doing the readings had given her cause for concern, and the doctor had done nothing to alleviate those concerns. Gail looked at the doctor sternly. "Do they want to send me home because they need more beds?"

The question went unanswered. Instead, he placed his hand on her forearm and rubbed gently. "You and your babies are my number one concern, and I will do nothing to jeopardize your well-being." Then he left without another word.

When Kerri returned to do her checks, she looked exhausted. The question seemed unnecessary, but Gail asked it anyway. "How is your day going?"

Kerri reached for Gail's chart. "Hectic."

The response did nothing to satisfy Gail. "Has it been hectic in a good way?"

Kerri never looked at Gail. "Things have just been hectic."

The response was unusually short coming from Kerri. Gail wanted to know more about the current situation and how it might affect her. "Is there a shortage of beds?"

Gail had to wait for an answer until Kerri had finished writing. "Other hospitals are feeling the crunch, but we are still doing fine."

The subtle shake of Kerri's head was all the answer that Gail needed to see. There must be a shortage, but until it concerned her, Gail was willing to play along. "That's good, but why do you look so exhausted?"

Kerri looked frustrated and almost emotional as she drew a deep breath and slowly exhaled. "We are short staffed, and everyone who has been able to make it to work has been overwhelmed with the increase in patients. We just can't give every patient the care and attention they need." She paused. "There is one scared little girl who will need someone with her at all times when she comes out of surgery."

Gail's concern about being released prematurely helped her formulate a plan to ensure she would be able to stay. "Bring the girl into my room when she is out of surgery, and I will watch her."

Kerri looked surprised for a moment before she shook her head slightly and took another deep breath. "We can't ask you to do that. You are in the hospital to rest. Your doctor would not approve."

"You don't have to ask me. I'm offering. As for the doctor, he said I was doing well enough to go home. So watching a little girl sleep should be no problem."

Kerri stood motionless, almost as if she was shocked that a patient would tell her what to do.

Before the silence went any longer, Gail said, "Go ask him!"

Kerri left and returned a short while later to confirm that Gail hadn't changed her mind and was still willing to share her room with the girl. Once Gail had made it clear that she wanted to watch the girl, Kerri started to arrange the room for the second bed, giving details about the new roommate as she worked. "The girl is approximately three years old. She has suffered serious injuries, mostly to the face and upper body." Kerri's expression was thoughtful. "She was injured because she wasn't properly secured in an approved car seat. The surgeons have done a lot for her, but that poor girl will need a lot more surgeries."

Hearing the condition of the girl brought several questions to mind, and Gail had to ask. "How are her parents doing?"

Kerri moved the last chair and examined her work. "I'm not sure how the parents are doing. They were taken to a different hospital."

This information surprised Gail. "Why would they do that?"

"They brought the girl here for the plastic surgeons on staff. They are the best in town."

Gail had many more questions but simply responded, "Oh."

Two hours later, the little girl was brought into the room. The sight of the small child, her body wrapped in bandages until all that remained visible was her bruised and swollen face, affected Gail for reasons even she was at a loss to explain. With no parents or family around for the child, Gail was prepared to care for the girl as if she were her own child.

"The girl's name is Lexie," Kerri said as she lightly touched the back of the sleeping girl's hand.

"Lexie. That is such a pretty name," Gail said as she joined Kerri beside the girl's bed. "She looks like an angel."

Over the next couple of weeks, when bad dreams caused Lexie to cry out in fear, Gail was there to comfort her until sleep returned. Gail's concern for the girl had grown after learning that her parents had been released from the hospital, and hadn't been heard from since. One night Lexie woke with a start and was almost inconsolable as she cried for her parents. Gail comforted the frantic little girl, who repeatedly pleaded, "Don't leave me!"

The fearful voice touched Gail's heart, and before it became impossible to speak from emotion, Gail said, "I'm right here." Gail then leaned forward to kiss the tiny forehead. "I will be here for you."

Early the next morning, Gail thought about what she could do to help Lexie overcome her fears. She looked at the last gift her husband, Wade, had brought. It was a family of stuffed dogs. The father was dressed as Santa, and the mother as Mrs. Claus. Each puppy was dressed as an elf and attached to the parents by a ribbon leash. Knowing how much Lexie liked to hold the puppies, Gail cut the ribbon leash to the girl's favorite—the white puppy with a black spot around the eye. As she placed the puppy in Lexie's arms, Gail said, "Hold the puppy when you are scared, and know that I will always love you." Once again Gail kissed the tiny forehead. "I will be here for you."

"Do you promise?"

Gail took her by the hand. "I promise, and I will always be here for you."

The puppy in her arms seemed to work because Lexie began to sleep through the night. Two days later, an orderly came to take Lexie to surgery. Lexie was frightened and upset when she had to surrender the puppy before they took her away. Gail took her hand and said, "I will be here for you, I promise."

After Lexie was gone to surgery, Kerri entered the room with a small bouquet of flowers and three balloons on ribbons. Gail saw the balloons and instantly thought of how much fun she and Lexie would have playing with them. When the nurses who followed began singing "Happy Birthday," Gail was embarrassed that she had forgotten that today was her birthday.

Kerri went to the closet, retrieved Gail's clothes, and laid them across the back of a chair.

"What's up?" Gail asked as a frightening thought came to her.

"You are being discharged," Kerri confirmed.

"It's the doctor's birthday present to you!" the nurses exclaimed in unison.

Suddenly, this became the worst birthday ever. Today's surprise from her doctor was worse than any surprise Wade had ever conceived, and he would be hard-pressed to beat this one. Gail folded her arms across the top of her baby bump in defiance. "What if I'm not ready to be discharged?"

Kerri handed the clothes to Gail. "The doctor says you are and has already signed the discharge papers."

It was obvious that Gail was in a foul mood when she emerged from the washroom fully dressed and ready to go. "This is the worst birthday ever, and I'm not happy." Gail handed the small stuffed puppy to Kerri. "Make sure you give this puppy to Lexie when she comes back!"

Before Kerri could respond, Gail took back the stuffed puppy and held it close to her heart. "On second thought, I will give it to her myself."

Wade arrived to take Gail home. "Are you ready to go?"

The look Gail gave Wade told him everything he needed to know before she began to speak. "I am not leaving this hospital until I see Lexie and say a proper good-bye." She looked at those with her in the room. "Consider this my birthday present to myself."

Gail sat quietly in the corner chair, playing with the frayed end of the small piece of ribbon attached to the puppy while she waited for Lexie to return. When Lexie was returned to the room and tucked into her bed, Gail went to her side.

"How are you doing, princess?" Gail asked as she watched Lexie struggle unsuccessfully to open her eyes. "I'm here for you like I said I would be." Tears fell from Gail's eyes as she softly said, "I love you."

Lexie never opened her eyes but had a peaceful expression on her face.

Gail swallowed hard. She placed the small puppy in Lexie's hand and then proceeded to gently rub her hand and forearm. Gail then placed her lips close to Lexie's ear. "The doctor says that I have to go home." Gail swallowed hard again. "So you need to take care of the puppy to help you remember just how much I love you."

Wade watched as Gail stood motionless beside Lexie's bed, letting her tears flow freely. He moved forward and stood beside Gail. Together they watched the sleeping girl.

"Hang in there, princess," Wade said as he reached to place his hand on Gail's. Several minutes passed in silence before Wade placed his arm around Gail's shoulder. "We need to go."

Gail reluctantly agreed and was starting to pull away when Lexie grabbed her hand and frantically cried out, "Don't leave me, Mommy!"

Chapter One

THE THICK, DARK CLOUDS and heavy drizzle that had settled over the region for the past week were finally beginning to disperse. Those still or already up at this early hour could see the occasional star in the dark, moonless sky. With the recent spike in break-ins and a traumatic home invasion still at the forefront of everyone's thoughts, the neighborhood was on edge, even with the increase of security patrols by the private security firm and the local police department. Local news broadcasts did little to help the situation, given the news anchors' catchphrase whenever the name of the community was mentioned: "a neighborhood under siege in an urban war."

The security officer had just completed another scheduled patrol and reported that everything was clear before he left the area. As the final glow from his headlights was absorbed into the darkness, a black sedan with dark tinted windows and the headlights turned off emerged from a side road. The car stopped a short distance from the Rollins residence, and the doors began to open, only to quickly and quietly close when the light in the upstairs bathroom came on. Unwilling to sit and wait, the driver drove away until the security patrol had completed the next scheduled pass. The car returned, and several bags were unloaded from the trunk before the car sped away. The man left behind made his way to the Rollins house with the bags under his arms and over his shoulders.

Within mere seconds of reaching the house, he had disarmed the security system and entered through the small garage door. Once everything was inside, the man set to work putting his plan into motion. Aided only by the light from the street lamps and the outside security systems, the intruder moved freely around the main floor and placed the various items he had brought with him in strategic locations. Once he was satisfied that the main floor was in order, he proceeded upstairs to the second floor, where the family was asleep in their bedrooms.

The first doorway to the left was the bedroom of the Rollins's teenage son, Jason. The man slowly turned the doorknob and pushed the door until it was open just enough for a smaller person to enter, at which point there was resistance and a crinkling sound like empty potato chip bags being crumpled. This minor setback deterred any further attempts to open the door lest it reveal his presence.

He continued along the hallway until he reached the doorway to the bedroom of the Rollins's six-year-old daughter, Amber. The door opened easily, and the subdued light from the window revealed the angelic face of the sleeping girl. He stood silently in the open doorway and watched her as he listened to the peaceful rhythm of her breathing. He then pulled the door closed but did not latch it, to avoid disturbing the girl.

Once inside the master bedroom where Gail Rollins was asleep, he methodically secured the cords to the four bedposts without disturbing her. When she began to toss restlessly and talk in her sleep, Wade Rollins stopped what he was doing, moved away from the bed, and silently watched and listened from the shadows. He knew better than to surprise his wife, but he couldn't resist the temptation. He waited until she had settled enough that he felt he could continue undetected. Once the cords were secured and everything appeared to be in order in the master bedroom, he returned to Amber's room. A few moments later, he returned and sat in the shadows, watching his wife's restless sleep.

Wade Rollins had been away on business and was due to return home in two days, which made this situation ideal for a surprise. He had heard the news and knew what had been happening and even now questioned whether his planned surprise was appropriate. Knowing that waking Gail with a start was a bad thing helped him decide to remain silent a while longer. He listened to her talking in her sleep and gathered from her words and the thrashing under the sheets that the dream wasn't a pleasant one, but he remained in the shadows, not wishing to make his presence known.

As he sat in silence, he looked at Gail past the cords tied to the bedposts and imagined her reaction to the pleasant surprise of his unexpected presence for her birthday. Gail had been disappointed when she found out that he would be away for her birthday but had known that there was nothing she could do to change it. Wade could envision the momentary look of disbelief followed by the little squeal of delight when Gail realized that he was home; he then thought of how special his birthday kiss would be.

As the predawn light slowly filtered into the room, Wade could more clearly see the features of the girl of his dreams and was glad to be home. He sat quietly and wished that she would awaken so that he could give her the hugs and kisses that had been sorely missed while they were apart. Gail meant the world to him, and he would stop at nothing to make her birthday special.

Over the years several events had transpired on or around her birthday that, if Gail were allowed to dwell on them, could cause her to become depressed on what should be a happy day. Wade was determined that this was not going to happen again this year. He had the entire day planned out to make sure she would have little or no time to dwell on her depressing thoughts. The sun was up, and the room was getting brighter. Wade was filled with anticipation because he knew it wouldn't be long before Gail awoke to see the balloons he had tied to the bedposts, and then he would give her a kiss before bringing her breakfast in bed.

His anticipation and excitement were hard to contain because once breakfast was over, he planned to take the family for a fun-filled day of activities to celebrate her birthday. Yes, he thought, as a result of his careful planning, today was going to be perfect and would give her absolutely no cause for concern.

Gail stirred slightly but was still asleep. Wade noticed that a dirty sock had somehow become attached to one of the balloon bundles. He slowly reached for the bright purple sock and gave a gentle tug to remove it. As the sock came free, so did one of the balloons, which floated lazily toward the ceiling and into the path of the rotating blades of the ceiling fan.

When the balloon popped, Gail sat upright in bed and gasped. "A gunshot!" she exclaimed as she fumbled for the edge of her sheets and looked about.

Wade felt bad that he had scared Gail and began to move toward her. He was still in the shadows when her eyes met his. She pulled the sheets tightly around her and gave a bloodcurdling scream. Gail grabbed the book that had fallen to her side as she read herself to sleep the night before and threw it at the head of the intruder, followed by the phone and then the clock radio.

Wade ducked the flying book and other projectiles and moved into the light as he made his way to her side. "Happy Birthday, sweetheart!" he sheepishly exclaimed.

Gail was glad to have Wade home for her birthday but made it abundantly clear that the less than stellar surprise to start the morning had been a bad idea. Their conversation on the matter ended with the reminder that she didn't like birthday surprises and his promise that he would never try anything like that again, ever!

Gail enjoyed the rest of the day and expressed her appreciation for his efforts. It was a memorable day so full of activities that the kids were exhausted at the end of it and went straight to bed after a light meal. She was glad the day had moved at such a hectic pace that she had never had time to entertain or dwell on those persistent negative thoughts and memories that had become an unwelcome part of her birthday.

But as the evening progressed, Gail was frustrated and annoyed with herself for allowing those negative thoughts that Wade had tried so valiantly to keep away to now occupy her mind. She forced herself to remain cheerful and act as if she was fine, but deep inside, she knew that it was too late, and by his actions it was apparent that Wade already knew. All doubt left when Wade entered the bedroom and without saying a word, came up to where she was seated at her make-up table, and started to massage her neck and shoulders. At that point she knew that he knew.

"A penny for your thoughts." Wade gently rubbed the back of her neck and worked on a knot until it released.

Gail sat in silence and enjoyed the attention from her husband. More than anything, she was glad he was home. She was so grateful to have this wonderful, caring man in her life and knew that Wade had tried his best to keep her depressing thoughts away all day. Right now she was embarrassed that he knew she had let them in. After he asked about her thoughts for a third time, she knew that she had to respond.

She wiped the tears from her eyes, and her head dropped even lower as she spoke. "I know it seems foolish after all these years, but right now I can't help thinking about Lexie."

Wade continued to rub her shoulders and then started to move down her back. "How many years has it been?"

Gail pretended to ponder the question, as if she needed time to find the answer she already knew. "Sixteen years."

Wade continued to rub gently and methodically. "Sixteen years is a long time to worry about a girl you may never see again."

Images of the injured girl wrapped in bandages flashed in her mind, and Gail became emotional as she softly replied, "Yes, it is, but I just can't stop thinking about her." Gail sensed a pressure change as Wade rubbed her back, and she knew that his frustration was growing because he was unable to make it right, and she was unable to let it go.

"Are you sure it's about Lexie and not about the promise you were unable to keep?" Wade finished rubbing her back and shoulders and sat next to his wife. "Are you at least over being upset with the doctor for discharging you on your birthday?"

Gail had figured out several years earlier that the doctor had discharged her at Wade's request as a surprise birthday gift. She knew that her husband had meant well, but he had underestimated her attachment to Lexie. She also knew that the doctor was a good friend of Wade, and over the years that friendship had been proven by his willingness to stand by the story that it had been his idea. Gail hoped that one day, when these troubling thoughts were behind her, the three of them could look back on this, share a good laugh, and maybe even refer to these as the good old days. "I'm over being upset with the doctor and my being discharged before I was ready. Not knowing how Lexie is doing, I may need a while longer to let the man responsible for the situation off the hook."

Gail watched Wade's reaction to her last comment and could only imagine how he must feel for creating the situation where the memories of Lexie would affect her. Unfortunately, they both knew that those weren't the only upsetting thoughts to appear on her birthday.

Wade started to unbutton his shirt. "So how are we doing on your thoughts of abandonment?"

"They are not thoughts of abandonment!" Gail smacked his leg with her hand. "You know perfectly well that I sometimes wonder about the circumstances surrounding my birth mother and her decision to give me up for adoption."

"Like I said, each year your birthday reminds you that she gave you away. You have stated several times that you feel she abandoned you."

Gail thought about her children and how sad she would be to not be there for them on those special days in their lives or when they needed her. She swallowed hard. "I don't feel abandoned. I just wonder sometimes if she thinks about me on my birthday or, for that matter, if she thinks of me at all."

The feeling of security she found in Wade's powerful arms was welcome as she snuggled next to the man she loved. He held her close and spoke softly. "I wish that you could be content with what you have and be happy for yourself." He kissed her forehead.

"I am happy!"

Wade remained silent a few moments before he spoke again. "Yes, you are—that is, until special occasions like your birthday and family times like Christmas come around. Then you become miserable because you feel that something is missing in your life."

"Is it really that bad?"

Wade kissed her forehead again. "Ever since your parents revealed that you were adopted, they say that you have been consumed by the overwhelming desire to find and meet your birth mother."

"I wouldn't say consumed, but I would like to meet her one day."

With Wade's prolonged silence, Gail wondered what he was thinking, but she chose to remain silent as well until he was willing to share his thoughts. The silence was broken by a big sigh from Wade. "I love you more than any words can express, and the very thought of disappointing you brings me pain. Over the years I have secretly tried to find answers that might bring relief from your recurring thoughts, but my efforts to find these people have been no more successful than yours. So when you suffer like this, I suffer in my own way."

"You have been looking? Why didn't you tell me?"

"I never wanted to get your hopes up and not be able to deliver." Wade excused himself and went to the den. He returned with some papers in hand. "I have used the vast resources available to me and many personal contacts in my attempt to find these people for you. Unfortunately, we are unable to bypass the privacy laws to locate Lexie and prove to you that she is not alone. As for finding our way past the legal roadblocks associated with closed adoptions, if a person doesn't wish to be found, or if someone doesn't want them found, there is a good chance that they may never be found."

Gail took the papers and found information that she had been unable to obtain, and yet there was still no success in the efforts to locate these people she wanted to find. She fought back her emotions because now more than ever, she didn't want Wade to think that he had disappointed her. "Where do we go from here?"

"We keep trying. We keep trying and continue to pray for divine intervention." Wade took the papers from Gail and placed them in his sock drawer.

When Gail spoke, it was in a soft, subdued voice. "You know how every night I pray that I might find relief from these memories and thoughts?"

"I think you may have mentioned that once or twice." Wade wrapped his arms around her shoulders and kissed the base of her neck.

Gail shook her head and placed her hands on his arms. "Well, last night during my prayers, I actually felt as if an answer came to me, but I'm not sure."

Wade gave a small squeeze followed by another kiss to the base of her neck. "What's not to be sure about?"

Gail was thoughtful and spoke quietly. "I'm not sure if the impression I felt was an answer to my prayer."

"What would make you doubt the impression received during your prayer?"

Gail lowered her head and raised her hands to her face. "I don't know what to think, but since that prayer I have felt compelled to plan a reunion with my family at our home for this Christmas."

Gail couldn't see Wade's expression but could imagine how it looked. She remembered the disaster that had been the last family reunion; by the end no one had been on good speaking terms. Yet now she was telling him that she felt compelled to plan another family reunion as an answer to her prayers. Whenever the topic of a family reunion came up, Wade would always say that compared to the task of keeping her family happy, Noah had it easy building the ark.

Wade asked, "So how long do you feel that this reunion should last, two or three days?"

Gail was thoughtful a few moments before responding. "I think it would be nice for the family to be together during the week before Christmas and remain as long after as they would be able to stay."

During the prolonged silence that followed, Gail could only imagine what Wade was thinking. Perhaps the prospect of having her family underfoot for more than two or three days scared him, and he was debating whether to quash the event or give his approval.

Wade broke his silence. "So what have you already planned, and how are you planning to keep your family happy for the week?" He paused. "More importantly, what is this going to cost?"

Gail avoided the question about the cost and outlined her plans to a silent Wade. It was only when she asked for his assurance that he would be at home to help for the week, and not tied up at work as he normally was when he wanted to avoid family, that he made a sound.

"Before you make more plans for the reunion, it would be wise to see if your family can come." Wade took her by the hand. "I don't want you to do all the planning and then be disappointed."

Gail agreed with Wade that she should make sure the family could come before she got her hopes up. She looked at the alarm clock and counted the hour time difference to where her brother Dale, a junior diplomat, was stationed. She found it odd that after all these years he was still only a junior diplomat, but deep down, she suspected that his love of practical jokes and occasional actions that showed a lack of maturity might have something to do with it. Gail was excited when she realized that if she called right now, she might catch him at his office. Better yet, she might have a chance to speak to Amanda, his assistant, who was about the nicest person she knew and who she felt would make a wonderful sister-in-law if her brother would stop being such a fool.

She dialed the number and waited impatiently. After the phone had rung several times, Gail was about to hang up when a sweet yet official-sounding voice answered and gave the scripted greeting.

"Hello. Amanda?" Gail said, almost feeling guilty that she was relieved to be speaking with Amanda instead of her brother Dale.

"Yes, and who am I speaking with?" Amanda asked cautiously.

"This is Gail Rollins, Dale's sister. How are you?"

"Fine," Amanda replied as the official sound in her voice melted away to a more casual tone.

"That's wonderful," Gail said quickly. "Can I ask you to do something for me?"

There was a noticeable pause. "Sure, I guess." There was another pause. "What's up?"

Gail considered telling Amanda that she was planning a surprise family reunion as a Christmas gift for her parents. The part about it being a gift for her parents wasn't exactly true, yet she thought this would sound better than the real reason. Besides, she knew that the reunion would definitely be a surprise for her parents. Gail decided to proceed with the truth and not try to hide her intent in half-truths.

She told Amanda how over the past few days she had felt that the family needed to have a reunion and was planning to host one at her house during Christmas. Just for good measure, she added that she thought the reunion would make a nice gift for her parents. Just as Gail had hoped, Amanda loved the idea of surprising her parents with the gift of family.

"I'll bet that you want to know if Dale's schedule will allow him to come," Amanda said. "Let me check his calendar." A moment later, with an almost apologetic tone in her voice, she informed Gail that as of right now his calendar showed an official invitation to a wedding that week, which would make it impossible for Dale to attend the reunion. "On the bright side, Dale is uncertain if he wants to attend and hasn't instructed me to return the RSVP. So there still might be a slim chance."

"A slim chance is better than none at all." Gail was relieved that there might actually be a chance of having Dale at the reunion.

"I'll do what I can to get him there. I must tell you that after the last family reunion he attended, I was instructed to say that he was too busy to ever attend another one." Amanda then took the time to share what she knew of his feelings about the last reunion, especially his feelings toward his brother and his brother's wife.

Gail knew that there had been some tension between the brothers, but not to the extent she was now hearing from Amanda. It hurt Gail deeply to think that Dale might let those bad feelings with Jerry keep him from being with the rest of his family for Christmas. Since the day she had found out she was adopted, Gail had been almost obsessed with being close to family. Yet here was her brother who would rather stay on the other side of the world from a loving family who missed him and then claim that it was his job that kept them apart.

Gail gave a big sigh as she realized that her efforts might be in vain, but she had to try. "I know that the last reunion ended badly, but it is important to me that the family be together for Christmas this year. I can't explain why, but if you could somehow manage to bring him to this side of the world, it would be greatly appreciated." She listened to the silence on the other end of the line. "You see, I'm adopted, and being with family is really important to me, so if you could help—"

Amanda broke in on Gail's sentence. "You're adopted?"

"Yes, I am." Gail was quite surprised by Amanda's reaction and wondered what had prompted it. She didn't have to wait long for the answer.

"I was adopted too, and I know exactly what you mean about family being important. My adoptive parents were killed in a car accident. I'm trying to find my birth mother so I can once again be part of a family," Amanda said as her normally controlled voice began to crack with emotion.

Gail gave her a few moments to compose herself before saying, "If my brother would come to his senses and ask you to marry him, you could be part of our family."

Amanda gave a soft cough before she spoke again. "Thank you for the vote of confidence, but I'm fairly certain that being number two in line for his heart isn't going to cut it." They talked some more about Dale and the mystery woman in his life. Amanda was fairly certain that she was the daughter of some ambassador, but it was hard to know which one. Several of the daughters liked Dale. They spoke a bit longer before Amanda said, "Here is what I can do for you about getting Dale to the reunion."

By the end of their conversation, Gail had Amanda's assurance that if it was at all possible, Dale would be at the reunion, but to make it easier for Amanda to arrange, Dale shouldn't know about the reunion until it was too late for him to make any changes to Amanda's arrangements.

Gail heard Dale's voice in the background—he must have just arrived back at the office—as Amanda told Gail not to worry and that she would call with the details when there were any. Amanda said good-bye and hung up the phone.

Gail hung up the phone and wiped a tear from her eye as she looked heavenward and said a little prayer. First, she asked that Amanda would be successful in finding her birth mother, and second, she asked that she could work her magic so that Dale would be with the family at Christmas.

Wade allowed Gail a few moments to compose herself and dry her tears before he asked, "So what's the verdict?"

Gail smiled as she wiped another tear. "A definite maybe for Dale to be here if Amanda can pull it off."

"What is Amanda going to pull off?"

Gail rubbed her hands together. "Amanda just has to make sure that there are no conflicting appointments that would prevent Dale from coming … that's all."

Normally, a phone call to her brother Jerry was an easy task that she looked forward to, but with the new insight about his relationship with Dale, she was hesitant to call him about a family reunion. Gail sat in front of her phone, her finger resting on the speed dial button. Thanks to Amanda, Gail was aware of Dale's feeling about the last reunion and how strong and negative they were. She also knew that her brother Jerry was even more passionate about things. If Dale felt strongly about not wanting another reunion, she could only imagine what Jerry would say when she asked.

Gail thought long and hard about what to say if the response from her brother was negative. She knew that she wanted to make the call, and she felt prompted to make the call, yet she hesitated, almost as if she feared she would find that her family had never liked each other.

She shrugged her shoulders and pulled her finger away from the phone as she considered ignoring the promptings—until she remembered just how long she had waited for an answer to her prayers. If she was to attain the desires of her heart, the least she could do was put forth the effort and prove her sincerity. If she expected to make the impossible happen, then she was going to do her part.

Gail finally pushed the button. She was going to invite Jerry and his family to her home during Christmas for either a fun-filled family reunion or the start of World War III.

There was no answer, which was a relief because this gave Gail a chance to better plan what she was going to say. After the beep Gail started talking. "It's Gail. I'll call back in the morning. Bye." She considered calling her parents, but at this hour they would be either out with friends or in bed trying to sleep. Either way, she was not about to leave just a message for them. "I'll call my parents and Jerry in the morning," she said. Gail slid between the sheets, barely giving Wade time to close his book before she turned out the light.

After a good night's rest, Gail made the calls. The first phone call was to her mother, and as the phone rang, Gail remembered that there had been no phone call from her parents to wish her a happy birthday the day before. Her mother answered. "Hello, Gail. How was your birthday?"

"It was good. Wade even made it back in time for my birthday."

"How wonderful. Were you pleasantly surprised?"

Gail knew how she wanted to answer, but she didn't have the time to fully discuss the details of Wade's surprise. They spoke for the better part of an hour, and Gail still hadn't extended the invitation. Before there was another change of topic, Gail said, "Wade and I would be honored if you spent Christmas with us at our house this year."

"That sounds wonderful, but your father and I might have other plans at Christmas. If we are in town, we will definitely be there."

She felt the enthusiasm leave her body as she listened to her mother's response. "I hope you can make it. You know how the kids love seeing you." Gail listened to see whether playing the grandchildren card would have any effect but sensed that it had failed. They talked a few minutes longer and then said their good-byes.

Gail hung up the phone and sat in silence, feeling that unless something changed, her family might never get together again. Before she could dwell on the subject any longer, Amber climbed onto her lap for a kiss and then to snuggle in her arms. Gail ran her fingers through the long, naturally curly blonde hair, which if cut short would curl into tight rings resembling a scouring pad. With her bright blue eyes and perfect lips that formed an endearing smile, this six-year-old resembled the fine porcelain dolls in Gail's doll collection. Gail held Amber close until she complained and squirmed to the floor. Aside from her stubborn nature and a willingness to call things as she saw them, Amber was perfect in every way.

Chapter Two

SEVERAL WEEKS HAD PASSED since Gail first talked to Wade about the prospect of having the reunion. Gail was relieved that the family reunion was actually going to happen in spite of the many obstacles that had arisen. Now all she needed was Amanda's call to confirm that Dale was on his way.

The phone rang, and Gail saw that it was Amanda. The call was earlier than expected, and she panicked, fearing that something had happened. She calmed herself and let it ring twice more. "Hello?"

"It's Amanda."

"And?" Gail asked.

"The plane just took off, and Dale is on his way to a conference that he never wanted to attend but has to go to since the registration was authorized and sent."

Gail was unsure what to make of this development, especially at this late hour. "Is that going to affect Dale coming to the reunion?"

The laugh on the other end gave Gail hope. "The conference puts Dale on your side of the world. Good fortune is yours because Dale received a wedding invitation from one of those ambassador's daughters that like Dale so much, and it seems he likes more than he is willing to let on. Attending the wedding will bring him right to your doorstep."

"So he will make it to the wedding and the reunion?" Gail asked.

"The wedding, yes." Amanda paused. "As for the reunion, I'm not sure."

"What do you mean?" Gail worried that all of her hard work might be slipping away.

Amanda waited for Gail to calm herself. "I told Dale about the reunion at the airport when he asked what hotel he was booked in. I told him that he was staying at your house for a family reunion and that you were expecting him to be there. That was just before he was to board the plane, and he never said another word to me." Amanda took a deep breath. "He seemed upset, and I think that I may have slipped from being number two in line for his heart. In fact, he may never speak to me again."

"You don't mean that, do you?" Gail feared the worst.

There was a brief silence. "You didn't see the look on his face."

"Don't worry about that. I promise that Dale will have a good time, and I will put in lots of good words for you." They shared a small laugh before they ended the call.

Gail appreciated what Amanda had done and hoped that once Dale was reunited with the family, he would forgive her deception. She hung up the phone and wondered what kind of mood Dale would be in if and when he arrived. She let the potential negative thought slip away since there was nothing she could do about it and continued her preparations for the reunion and for Christmas.

The phone call from her parents confirming they would be in town for Christmas hadn't made Gail feel as happy as it should have. Obviously, she was no better at planning surprises than Wade was. Gail thought about her mother's phone call and how her parents hadn't masked their disappointment that their other plans had fallen through. She looked at the meal she had prepared to freeze for the reunion. It was her mother's favorite, and Gail wondered if she had prepared this dish to ease her mother's disappointment—disappointment that Gail knew she was responsible for.

Her brother Jerry had been adamant about not coming to the reunion when Gail had first contacted him. He never mentioned anything about Dale; instead, he stated that his work overseas for an oil company kept him from his own family, and when he was home, he enjoyed time alone with his wife and son. Gail was relieved when he called back later to say that he'd had a change of heart and he and his family would be coming. Gail wasn't sure what had caused his change of heart, but she suspected that he wanted to avoid having their parents at his house four Christmases in a row. Whatever the reason was, it didn't matter because the reunion was set.

With the reunion now only days away, Gail was intent on not being stuck in the kitchen while the rest of the family visited. She was preparing the final meal to place in the freezer when Gail remembered the subtle and not-so-subtle hints from Wade about serving simple, inexpensive snack foods buffet-style during the reunion. His advice was making more and more sense as she looked at the feasts in the freezer, but this was her family, and if the event was to be memorable, she had to do it right.

She placed the last dish in the freezer with all of the Christmas baking. Gail admired all the cookies and tarts as she closed the door with a firm but gentle push. Standing tall, she stretched her lower back and then pushed an annoying lock of hair from her face. Gail smiled as she patted the freezer door and visualized the joyful reactions of her family as they enjoyed the meals and the baked treats. She also imagined Wade's reaction and comments about the cost.

A muffled thump from the other room brought Gail's thoughts back to the present, and she went to check out the source. In the living room Amber was replacing the flower pot on the end table with a new poinsettia, trying to make the plant stand straight and tall without any dirt in the pot. Gail saw Amber make a quick, nervous glance at the pile of dirt on the carpet and then at the wounded plant. She smiled as

Amber turned and ran to her with outstretched arms to give her an enthusiastic hug and kiss.

"I love you, Mommy!" shouted Amber as she wrapped her arms tightly around Gail's neck. "Can we have some cookies and a glass of milk?" Amber began pulling Gail from the room by her fingers.

Two tall glasses of milk were soon on the table, and Gail went to the pantry for the new bag of Amber's favorite peanut butter cookies. She reached to where the bag was supposed to be and stopped when she saw that the peanut butter cookies were missing. In fact, most of the cookies and chips were missing, including a tray of Christmas cookies. Closing the pantry door firmly, Gail returned to the table empty-handed.

"The cookies we were going to have are missing." Gail placed the two glasses of milk in the refrigerator. "I think I know where they are, and if we're lucky, they haven't all been eaten." The look of disappointment on Amber's face made it hard for Gail to keep a straight face. Gail fought to hold back a smile. "You run along to the living room and clean up the dirt while I look for the cookies."

Amber raised her hands in a small shrug. "What dirt? You just finished cleaning the living room."

Gail smiled at her little angel with the big blue eyes and curly blonde hair. "The dirt on the floor from the plant you were trying to make stand straight when I came into the room."

The innocent smile left Amber's face as she realized that her attempted cover-up had already been discovered.

"You take the small vacuum cleaner into the living room, and I'll help you clean up once I speak to your brother." Gail handed Amber the small handheld vacuum cleaner and gave her behind a small swat to get her moving.

Standing in the hallway outside of Jason's door, Gail listened briefly to the muffled sound of his favorite movie playing. She knocked softly at first and then a little louder until she heard that all-important response giving her permission to enter Jason's personal domain. She pushed the door open against the resistance from the dirty clothes piled behind the door. Gail could see that the movie was playing to her son's back as he intently played a computer game. On the floor beside the computer desk was an assortment of empty bags from previously enjoyed snacks. Scanning the room, she saw a partial glass of milk on the end table and the missing bags of cookies.

Entering the room was quite the challenge for Gail because of the substantial resistance put up by the piles behind the door. "I do wish that you'd take more pride in the way your room looks and clean it up," Gail said, forcing the door open.

Jason didn't look up from the computer. "I just did a cleanup and put the dirty clothes behind the door where you told me to." He turned his head from the computer screen just long enough to make eye contact as he spoke in a firm tone. "I'll finish the cleaning so that you won't throw out something important."

Gail remembered the reaction from the last time she had cleaned his room, when she threw out the smelly dish with a healthy growth of mold that just happened to be his science project. She looked at the piles of old papers and napkins on the dresser and computer desk. As she reached for the bag of peanut butter cookies, Gail wondered what, in all of this mess, could be considered important.

With cookies in hand, Gail carefully left the room and joined Amber in the living room. She helped her scoop the dirt from the carpet and into the flower pot to support the plant. Then they vacuumed before having their treat of milk and cookies.

The rest of the day passed without any further incident, and Gail actually found time to sit and read from the newest book by her favorite author. But she was unable to become totally immersed in her reading because she kept stopping to think of the upcoming reunion and whether there was something she might have forgotten. Gail could scarcely contain her excitement over her good fortune in having the entire family over for Christmas, but the excitement was tempered by the burning question of how this reunion was going to help her.

Chapter Three

THE KNOWLEDGE THAT HER home and family would be on display during the reunion pushed Gail to clean tirelessly. Her house was less than a year old and should have required only surface cleaning for the event, but she even went so far as to clean and organize the closets. She tired of Jason's poor responses to her requests that he clean his room, and much to his very vocal displeasure, she took it upon herself to spend a whole day doing it for him while he was with friends. She disposed of three large bags of garbage in the process and could have filled more.

Now it was the morning of the big day, and in a few short hours the family would arrive for a much-anticipated week of togetherness. Gail lovingly applied the finishing touches to the various seafood dishes she had prepared for the arrival meal and placed them carefully in the refrigerator. A quick check of the pantry confirmed that the crackers were still in adequate supply for the evening since Jason's last trip to the kitchen.

As Gail moved around the house, checking for any details that might have been missed, she came upon Amber in the living room looking at and playing with the decoration on the end table. This small decoration was a family of stuffed dogs dressed up to look like Santa and Mrs. Claus, with two puppies dressed up as elves. Amber's small fingers were playing with the frayed end of a ribbon that had been cut. Gail sat with her daughter, and they looked at the dogs together as Gail arranged them to how they had been positioned before Amber picked them up. They sat in silence for a few precious moments, both admiring the dogs, until Amber asked, "Mommy, why did Jason do it?"

"Do what?"

With a comical sigh that Gail supposed was an attempt to show frustration. Amber held the small ribbon in her fingers. "Why did he cut the ribbon and lose the other puppy? The family could be together if we still had the puppy." She looked at Gail with her big blue eyes. "Do you know where the puppy is so we can fix the ribbon and make the family all better?"

Gail took Amber in her arms and kissed the top of her forehead. Gail rocked with Amber awhile before saying, "Jason never cut the ribbon. I did, a long time ago."

"Do you know where the other puppy is?" Amber's voice was filled with excitement. "If you do, then we can fix the family and make it right." The look in her daughter's eyes told Gail that anything less than the puppy on the end of the ribbon was going to disappoint her.

Gail thought hard about the best way to tell the story of the missing puppy so that there would be no unanswered questions when it was over. Clearing her throat, Gail began. "Before Jason was born, Mommy had to spend a lot of time in the hospital to make sure he was going to be healthy." She paused and fought back a tear. "Do you remember when we told you that your older brother was a twin?"

Amber looked up. "Do you mean that he was something other than a boy?"

Gail smiled when she realized that Amber had never understood what twins were. "Jason has always been a boy. Twins means that there were two babies in Mommy's tummy, not just one. In fact, your daddy bought this dog family because the two smaller puppies looked the same, like twins, and we were expecting two babies."

The look of uncertainty and concern on Amber's face was unexpected and troubling to Gail. "What's the matter?"

23

"Was the other baby bad, and that's why you never brought him home?" Amber had tears welling up in her eyes, her little fingers still playing with the small ribbon.

Gail could see that this was starting to go badly, and she had only just begun. Hugging Amber close to her, Gail said in a soft, reassuring voice, "The baby wasn't bad, sweetheart." Gail was hesitant to tell her daughter that the other baby had lived only a few days. "We were only able to bring Jason home."

The look on Amber's face changed from one of concern to one of disgust as she sat tall and pulled away from Gail. "You gave a baby away?" There was silence in the room before Amber's next question. "How could you?"

Gail was shocked and speechless, with no response to give.

"So did you give the puppy away with the baby?"

This was going very, very badly and in a big hurry, just as Gail had feared it might when she began the explanation. Her daughter's vivid imagination had taken over, and the air was filled with questions that, once answered, would lead to even more questions. Holding Amber close, Gail waited for her to calm down and stop asking more questions before attempting to provide answers to those already asked. First, she had to eliminate the imaginary and bring the conversation back to reality. Taking a deep breath, Gail assured Amber that the other boy had not been given away as a baby but had returned to live with his Heavenly Father. Once she felt that Amber understood and was accepting of that point, it was time to deal with the cause of the whole discussion—why the ribbon had been cut and the puppy taken from its family.

Gail felt like a criminal making a confession under the constant stare of her daughter. She began once again to deliver the explanation. "The reason I cut the ribbon and took the puppy from the dog family was to give a small frightened girl a gift to make her feel better."

"Who was the girl? Do I know her? Are we related? Can I play with her?" Amber asked in rapid-fire succession.

Gail held an index finger to her lips and motioned for Amber to be quiet. "She was a little girl who had been in a bad car accident. You don't know her because she is older than your brother, and I doubt that the two of you would want to play together. As for being related, I think not," Gail said in a loving voice.

"Can we ask her to give the puppy back now that she is grown up?"

Gail hugged Amber and gently rubbed her arm. "How can I ask Lexie to return the puppy when I don't know where she lives? Besides, she may have lost it by now. It has been quite a few years since I gave it to her."

"I still have all my gifts from you. So I'm sure that she still has the puppy." It was quite apparent that for Amber the thought of losing a gift was absurd. "Maybe Daddy can find out where she is so we can ask her for the puppy."

This mother–daughter moment ended when a loud crash came from the kitchen. Gail slid Amber from her lap and rushed to check it out. To her surprise all appeared to be in order, and she could only wonder what had caused the noise. Gail heard the refrigerator's open-door alarm beep and walked across the kitchen to push the door closed. She pushed and heard the sound of rubbing, grating glass. A sinking feeling came over her when she opened the door and saw the glass from the broken bowls mixed in with the seafood dishes.

Gail dropped to her knees and reached into the mass of lovingly prepared food and tried to salvage what she could. She soon realized that this was a futile effort since the destruction had been complete. Every one of the dishes was unfit for human consumption, with small pieces of glass everywhere.

When she removed a dish from the back right-hand corner of the refrigerator, Gail was certain that she knew what had happened. Stuck in the middle of what used to be a crabmeat dip were the broken remains of one of the special crackers she had purchased for the party. There was little doubt in her mind about what had happened and who was responsible for the disaster. But the party was hours away, and now was not the time to deal with Jason.

Gail began to call her suppliers in hopes of being able to recover and make some of the dishes again. With each phone call, she became less and less optimistic about being able to rebuild the meal. All of the suppliers were telling her the same thing: "All of our stocks are depleted. We have some but not all of what you have asked for."

Gail was in shock because her perfectly planned event was about to crash and burn before it even began. In the face of imminent disaster, her thoughts now turned to her son Jason, who it seemed had disobeyed her by sampling the food. As Gail planned the demise of her son, she remembered the girl Jason secretly had a crush on but with whom he would never risk more than social encounters at his father's company functions. The girl worked with her father, who catered the events. Gail rushed to Jason's room and knocked. She listened to the sound of rustling paper and knew that the room was occupied. She knocked again, only this time much louder, and was quite insistent. "Jason, open up. I know you're in there!"

Gail opened the door and looked toward the sound. To her surprise, the noise was from the efforts of her own little dog as he licked the last crumbs from the bottom of a large potato chip bag. The room looked as if Jason had left in a hurry but didn't want to miss his movie or lose his computer game since they were both paused. It almost seemed as if Jason was hiding from her. She quickly dropped to her knees and checked under the bed to see if he was hiding there like he had when he was younger. Nothing was under the bed but a pair of smelly running shoes and the unwashed lucky socks he wore for playing basketball.

While she was busy looking under the bed, Jason appeared in the room. "Are you cleaning again? Didn't you do enough damage last time you cleaned?" Jason removed the corner of the bedspread from her hand and allowed it to fall gently to the floor. "What are you looking for?"

Gail stood up from her knees. "I was looking for you."

Jason laughed as he stood to his full stature, which was two inches taller than his father. "I won't be hiding under that bed anymore. I barely fit on top of it." His smile was cautious when he asked, "Why are you looking for me?"

Gail made good eye contact with Jason and clenched a fist behind her back. She dug a fingernail into the palm of her hand to distract herself from the mental image of her hands closing around his neck.

"It would seem that the top shelf in the fridge came loose, and now all of the food for tonight is ruined—full of small pieces of glass mixed in with the food." It required all of her self-control to remain calm while Jason acted as if the news of the ruined food was a complete surprise to him, even though she knew he was fully aware of the damage.

Jason sat down in front of his computer. "So why are you looking for me?" He reached for the mouse and then stopped and turned to Gail with a look of disbelief. "You think that I had something to do with it, don't you?"

Gail never flinched. "What happened to the food is not my immediate concern. Finding replacement food for tonight is." She matched the intensity of Jason's stare with her own. "I need to know the name of the catering company your father uses."

Jason held his ground and never broke eye contact. "And what makes you think that I would know this? I only go for the food. What truck it comes in and who brings it is of no concern to me." Jason handed Gail the phone. "I honestly have no idea what the company name is. You should call Dad."

Gail took the phone. "I was hoping to avoid disturbing him so that he can finish his work and come home early."

"If you want the information, you need to call Dad."

Gail remained calm but was becoming frustrated at the lack of help. "I know that you have a crush on the caterer's daughter, and she seems to like you." She watched Jason blush. "So I had hoped that you would have a name and number that I could call."

An almost sinister smile came to Jason's lips. "I did have a phone number. Why, I even had a paper with the company name on it."

Gail was perplexed by his response. "What do you mean that you *did* have that information? Where is it now?"

With an impish grin Jason motioned toward the dresser. "All the information you need about the company was on one of the many small pieces of paper that used to be on my dresser."

"What do you mean, used to be?"

"They used to be right there until you cleaned my room." He motioned toward the chest of drawers with a few new papers on top. "I would love to help, but you threw out the blue napkin that had the company name and logo on the front and Vicki's name and home phone number written so beautifully on the back."

Gail felt her knees weaken. She was shocked to think that one of the crumpled pieces of paper she had cleared from the room, thinking it all to be of little value, would now mean so much to her. "Is there anything at all that you can remember about the company? Can you remember the color of the truck, the logo, anything at all?"

Jason became more serious. "The only thing I remember is that the company logo is an angel on top of a cake."

"An angel on top of a cake—are you sure about that?" Gail began to feel hopeful that Jason would come through.

Jason smiled. "Yes, I'm positive. I remember asking Vicki if the angel on the napkin was a picture of her because she looked so divine."

Gail fought the urge to laugh at what Jason had said; she knew that would be a bad idea when she saw Jason's peaceful look. "She is a lovely young lady. Do you remember the name of the company?"

"I'm sorry, but I have no idea what the company name is." He moved some papers on his desk as if he felt there was a chance he might find a clue. Jason stopped and looked at her. "You need to call Dad, but you need to hurry before all the stores are closed."

Without any further hesitation, Gail dialed the number to Wade's office. After three rings, she felt some uncertainty. Had Wade already finished and started on his way home? Was he out of the office in some back room, away from the sound of the phone? The phone rang several times before Wade answered.

"Hello?" Wade puffed into the mouthpiece.

"Hi, sweetheart. It's me," Gail said and waited for his breathing to slow. "I realize that you are really busy, but I have a situation."

"And what might that situation be?"

"Tonight's meal is ruined, and I need a miracle."

"What happened?"

"I'll tell you later. Right now I need the name and phone number of the caterer you always use." Gail had hoped for a quick answer and was ready with pen in hand.

What started as a short hesitation stretched into a long silence before Wade spoke. "I honestly don't know."

"How can you use a company as much as you use this one and not remember the name of it?"

Wade was slow to respond but managed to answer before Gail asked the question a second time. "My secretary arranges events like that. I just pay the bill."

"Let me speak to her. I'm in a hurry. Is she there?"

"No, she isn't. I gave her the day off."

After a long silence, Gail said tersely, "Call her!"

Wade protested mildly about not wanting to disturb her until his loving wife reminded him of what he had said before leaving the house that morning. "You told me that you couldn't take the day off to help me because the entire staff would be at the office, and you needed to be there as well."

"I do need to be here." Wade sounded defensive.

Gail needed the name and number and was feeling the pinch for time. "I don't doubt that you feel the need to be there. It just seems strange that the most important person in the entire process was given the day off." Having said her piece, Gail waited for a response.

"I'll call you right back."

A few minutes later Wade called back. Gail was happy to have the information, but she wasn't quite finished with Wade. "Quit being such a Scrooge and let your staff go home to be with their families." There was no response from Wade, so she continued. "Allowing for bad luck with traffic lights, you should be home with your family in half an hour as well." Gail hoped that she hadn't been too subtle or left any doubt as to when Wade was expected home.

Gail called the number Wade had given her.

"Thank you for calling Angelo's Catering Service. How may I help you?"

"I need to speak with Angelo about some food."

"I'm sorry, but we are closing now, and you will have to call back after Christmas."

Beyond asking how she could help, the girl proved to be of little help at all. Gail refused to accept the girl's position and demanded to speak with Angelo. Gail heard a distinct sigh.

"Angelo is on another line and has been talking with the customer for over thirty minutes. I have no idea how much longer he will be."

Gail didn't want to let go of her last fleeting hope. "I don't care how long I have to wait. I wish to speak with Angelo." Before being placed on hold, she mentioned that her husband was an extremely good customer, and her wishes needed to be respected.

Gail found herself on hold long enough to develop a distinct distaste for the programming selections of the radio station used for background music. Elevator music had more appeal. Soon the music was cut off, and Angelo answered.

"Thank heavens I caught up with you before you closed," Gail said with relief in her voice. "This is Gail Rollins, Wade Rollins wife. I have a family gathering, and all of the food I had prepared was destroyed when my son sampled it."

Angelo chuckled. "Jason does like to eat. I've seen him in action. I would like to help, but I am out of the supplies needed to create Wade's regular order."

Gail's voice changed from desperation to disappointment. "Do you have anything?"

Angelo paused. "I do have a food order here from a last-minute cancellation, but it may not be satisfactory for your function."

"What kind of food is it?"

Angelo sighed. "It's a complete feast of authentic Mexican dishes that we were to serve at a wedding reception."

"I'll take it!" Gail was surprised at her lack of sympathy for the couple's misfortune that had made the food available, but her main concern was the reunion. "Bill the food to my husband's account." Gail paused. "Can you still deliver?"

"Mrs. Rollins, with the cancellation my delivery people have all gone home, and you will have to find a way to pick up the food." Angelo excused himself briefly to speak with another person. When he returned, he said, "It seems that if Jason is home, my daughter would be happy to deliver the food. Is he home?"

"Yes, he is." Gail was excited at her good fortune but remembered her manners. "Thank you so much for your help, and tell Vicki that Jason will greet her when she arrives."

Angelo confirmed the address, and Gail heard him say away from the phone, "Jason's mother says that he will greet you when you arrive." Moments later, Angelo chuckled and confirmed, "Vicki is on her way."

"Thank you so much."

"You're welcome, and I hope the rest of the reunion goes smoothly."

"I'm sure it will." Gail was about to hang up when her curiosity got the better of her. "Do you know why the wedding was canceled?"

Angelo hesitated. "I do know a little bit of the story, but I don't know if I should tell."

Gail wasn't about to pry. If Angelo didn't want to reveal the circumstances of her good fortune, she was all right with that. She was surprised when Angelo chuckled and proceeded to tell all that he knew.

"It would seem that the bridal party was having a party in the groom's room without inviting the bride."

"Oh my," Gail gasped. "That doesn't sound good."

"No, it wasn't." Angelo chuckled again. "When the bride slipped into his room to wish him a good night, he was busy kissing the maid of honor."

"Ouch!"

"I'll say ouch. Not only was that party over, but so was the wedding."

Gail could only shake her head. "The poor girl must have been devastated."

"Oh, I think she was. I heard that she ordered everyone at the party to leave. Then she ran down the hall to her room, slammed the door shut, and locked it."

"The poor thing. Is she doing all right now?"

Angelo was more reserved than before. "They're not sure since she refuses to come out until after she speaks with the person she sent for."

"Who did she send for?"

"Don't know for sure, but it's definitely not her priest."

When Angelo finished the story, Gail had a smile on her face. "Thank you for sharing the story with me."

"It was my pleasure."

It was Gail's turn to chuckle as another question came to mind. "Do you think it would be appropriate to send a thank-you note to the groom?"

Angelo gave a hearty laugh. "I'm pretty certain that would be inappropriate. Enjoy your reunion."

Gail hung up the phone and breathed a sigh of relief. She shook her head and softly muttered, "Men!"

Gail debated whether she should tell Jason that Vicki was coming. She decided against it, thinking that it would be a nice surprise for Jason when Vicki arrived. She simply told him to clean up and put on his good clothes. Jason started to protest but stopped short when Gail glared and stated, "Do it!"

Gail remembered that she had left the living room before finishing her talk with Amber. Looking quietly around the corner, Gail saw Amber where she had left her. Only this time, instead of simply touching the frayed end of ribbon with her fingers, Amber was holding the small figures close to her heart and rocking them as she did her dolls. It was a touching sight, and Gail had no idea what to say or do in response. The clock in the hall chimed the regular announcement of the hour, and Gail began to panic slightly. It was later than she had realized, and she still had to clean up. Gail glanced at the clock and noted that it had been thirty-seven minutes since she had last spoken with Wade, and he still wasn't home.

From the bottom of the stairway, Gail was greeted by a sight that she would have expected on Halloween, but not at Christmas. Waiting for her at the top of the stairs was Jason, in an outfit she was sure he had planned to gain a reaction from her. He was wearing his baggy skateboarding shorts, the back side of which was torn and worn thin from the shorts' many introductions to concrete. His shirt was one that he had rescued from the rag bin because it had some sort of sentimental value. It may have had sentimental value, but it also had more holes than it did fabric to cover his body, and the solitary dark hair on his chest was looking very conspicuous and lonely.

Not wanting to spoil the surprise of Vicki coming to see him when the food was delivered, Gail tried numerous ways to convince Jason to change his clothes without telling him who was coming. She was about to ruin the surprise and tell him when the front doorbell rang. It was too late. Jason, in all his rebellious glory, raced down the stairs past Gail. With a large grin on his face, he cleared his throat and practiced a mocking bow, complete with the long sweeping motion of the hand to bid the visitor welcome. Gail tried to stop him, but that made him move that much faster.

He pulled the door open while making the long sweeping gesture. "Welcome to our nuthouse." When his eyes finally made contact with the person at the door, he stopped instantly and stood motionless, with his jaw dropped. There standing before him with a large box in her arms was the lovely Vicki.

Vicki's amusement was evident as her eyes moved from the purple spiked hair on his head to his very visible neon striped socks and mismatched running shoes. "Is your mother home?" Vicki shifted the heavy box and moved closer to the open door. "I brought the food she ordered for the party tonight."

Jason was paralyzed with embarrassment and unable to move. Gail moved her son to one side and took the box from Vicki. "Thank you so very much for bringing this over to me on such short notice. Excuse me while I set the table."

Vicki rubbed her right arm after the box was taken from her. "Would you like to help me bring in the rest of the food?"

Without saying a word, Jason obediently followed Vicki. As they made the trips from the van to the house, Jason began to speak more openly with Vicki, who was perfectly polite and careful not to add insult to an already injured ego.

"This must be some kind of party for your mother to want this much food."

Jason smiled. "We're having a family reunion—my mother's Christmas present to herself."

Vicki made no attempt to hide that she was admiring Jason's muscular chest. Jason blushed and folded his arms in an attempt to cover some of the holes in his shirt.

Vicki looked away and then into Jason's eyes. "Do you have a lot of family coming?"

"Not really. Ours is a small family. My grandparents are coming, plus my one uncle with his wife and their kid and my other uncle, the diplomat. Why do you ask?"

Vicki patted the boxes stuffed in the front entry. "There is enough food in these boxes to feed one hundred people. Do you want me to take some back to the store?"

Jason smiled and took Vicki by the hand. "My mother will find a place for the food. It will give her something to do besides telling me how to act when the family arrives."

Vicki giggled. "You dressed like this to annoy your mother tonight, didn't you?"

Jason glanced back over his shoulder to make certain that his words would be heard only by Vicki. "I had hoped that it was my uncle Dale at the door."

Vicki nodded to show her understanding. "Aren't you just a little bit happy that it was me at the door?"

Jason was still learning the art of keeping his foot out of his mouth when talking with girls, but even he could see that this was a time to proceed with caution. "I'm always happy to see you."

"So why have you kept me waiting all these months for a phone call that never comes?"

Jason swallowed hard. He frantically searched for an answer to get himself off the hook. "It … it's actually my mother's fault." He thought this was a good answer.

As Vicki looked at him silently with a puzzled expression, he began to doubt how good it was.

He quickly tried to explain further. "My mother cleaned my room and tossed out a pile of papers with names and numbers on them from the top of my dresser, including the napkin with your number on it."

Vicki feigned being hurt. "Were those other names and numbers for girls?"

Jason now wished he had taken more time to think as Vicki seemed to delight in watching him squirm.

"You're kind of cute when flustered." Vicki had a twinkle in her eye as she winked. "If you promise to be a good boy and call me, I'll give you my number again."

Jason wished for a power failure at that moment to hide the red flush of color that he knew was racing to his face. To keep Vicki from seeing the effect she was having on him, Jason raised her hand to his lips and kissed it.

Now it was Vicki's turn to blush. She stepped back out of the light and onto the step. "I have a dance rehearsal to be at. I should go."

"Let me walk you to your van." Jason took her by the hand as they walked side by side. "Thank you for coming by. It was nice."

"It was a lucky and enjoyable coincidence that my dance rehearsal is close to your house." Vicki climbed into the van. Jason closed the door carefully behind her. He bade her good-bye and watched from the sidewalk as she drove out of sight.

Jason returned to the house and softly closed the door before collapsing against the wall in the front entry with his head buried in his hands. The door to the garage opened, and Wade almost tripped over Jason and the boxes.

"What's going on in here?" Wade asked as he squeezed past Jason. "What's in the boxes?" Wade looked at Jason with his colorful hair and interesting clothing selection. "What are you supposed to be?"

Raising his head from his hands, Jason looked at his father. "I want to be invisible!"

"That's pretty hard to do with an outfit like that." Wade giggled, and Jason tried to hang his head even lower. Wade opened the top flap of the closest box to reveal the containers of food. "Are these boxes from Angelo?"

Jason nodded without raising his head from its resting place.

"Were they delivered by the lovely Vicki?"

There was no need for a verbal response; Jason's simple action of covering the back of his head with his hands gave the answer.

"Did she like your outfit?"

Jason raised the index finger of his right hand and pointed it at his father as he struggled to find the words that would express his feelings. Before any words could leave his lips, the doorbell rang, which brought the rest of the family to the entryway.

"What's with all these boxes?" Gail asked as she came up against the wall of cardboard. "I already took the food to the kitchen."

Jason shook his head as he stood and wiped the tears from his face. He opened the door. There once again stood Vicki with a package in her hands.

Vicki directed her words past Jason to Gail. "I found these in the van and debated whether I should bring them to you."

"What are they?"

"These are the dishes of hot peppers that were to go on the tables with the food—more as a decoration than a food because they are so hot, but they were part of the order."

Gail shrugged her shoulders. "If they are part of the order, I'll take them. What's with all these other boxes?"

Vicki smiled sweetly. "There were one hundred guests invited to the wedding reception. Dad told me that you wanted all of it for your party, and here it is."

Jason smiled because it was Gail's turn to drop her jaw and stare with mouth open at the boxes. Wade found the humor in the situation and started to laugh.

"What's so funny?" demanded Gail as she swatted Wade on the arm.

Wade brought his thumb and index finger to his nose and pinched. "I'll need to buy some air fresheners for the house by the time your family has eaten Mexican food for a week. I wonder if they make industrial-strength air fresheners for home use."

Jason was grateful when his parents each grabbed a box of food and left him alone with Vicki. He was even more grateful when Vicki started to speak. "I'm glad I forgot to leave the hot peppers earlier."

He was intrigued. "Why are you glad that you forgot?"

Vicki wrung her hands. "I wanted to ask if you would come to my dance recital tomorrow."

The invitation surprised him, but without hesitation Jason said, "It will be my pleasure."

Vicki thanked him with a small kiss on the cheek. "It is a dress-up affair. You should wear the nice suit you wore to the last company function."

"Why that suit?"

"It makes you look hot, and the other girls will be so jealous to see me with such a good-looking guy."

Jason felt the blood rushing to his face. He could see that Vicki was enjoying herself. "I will make you proud of me," he said as he reached for her hand as if to kiss it again, only to pull her close and give her a small kiss on the cheek.

The glow of her cheeks matched that of Jason's as Vicki made her exit. She stopped just long enough to tell him what time she would come by to pick him up.

Chapter Four

THE TIME FOR PREPARATION was past. Gail hoped that she hadn't forgotten any details and that they were ready for family to arrive. The Christmas decorations were hung in all the right places, and even the dog family was still on display, despite the feelings of uncertainty Gail had about Amber's fixation on the missing puppy. The first to arrive were Gail's parents, their arms loaded with gifts for Gail's family. Gail took the packages and handed them to Wade before greeting her mother and father with a big hug and a kiss.

Gail could scarcely contain her excitement while she waited for the others to arrive. Her mother would be so surprised. Gail was the perfect host in spite of the hurt she felt when her mother made no effort to mask her disappointment that Jerry had already made plans for Christmas. Gail was tempted to quiet the mumbling by telling her mother that the entire family was coming for the holiday. She was tempted, but after all the efforts to keep the reunion a secret from her parents, she decided to let it remain a surprise.

Her father grew tired of the continual complaints voiced by his wife and started to wander about the house. He was the first to venture into the dining room and discover that the food was not the usual seafood creations. He called his wife to him. "Look at the food Gail is planning to serve this evening." He lifted the various lids from the dishes and breathed deep. After smelling all the different aromas the dishes had to offer, he nudged his wife. "I told you that we shouldn't have stopped to eat. This food looks wonderful, and not a trace of fish to be found."

Gail's mother swatted him on the arm with the back of her hand. "Shush! Not so loud."

"What are you worried about? We're the only ones in here right now except for Amber, and she has no idea what I just said." He rubbed his arm lightly. "I was simply pointing out to you that our daughter is not going to feed us the same fish dishes she always does. You were concerned about nothing." He lifted the lid from the closest dish and inhaled deeply again. "This food reminds me of being in Mexico, and now, because I ate with you earlier, I may not be able to enjoy all of it. I can't see there being a whole lot of leftovers, at least not as much as there would have been with the fish."

Gail entered the room, having successfully directed the placement of luggage in the room reserved for her parents. "Your bags are in your room, and your coats are in the hall closet." She placed a stack of plates on the table. "Help yourselves. Enjoy!"

The doorbell rang. Gail went to the door and greeted her youngest brother Jerry, his wife Lisa, and their three year old son Brandon with a hug and a kiss. The parcels and gifts went under the tree while Jason and Wade carried the luggage up to their room.

Gail's mother was in awe and looked as if she might cry as she stood with her mouth open at the sight of Jerry and his family. "So this is why you refused to invite us to your home for Christmas."

Jerry nodded and bent down so his mother could greet him with a hug and a kiss. "We wanted our visit to be a surprise." He smiled. "Are you surprised?"

Gail showed them to the dining room, where they looked at the feast on the table. Gail excused herself to bring the pitcher of ice water to the table. Her mother followed close behind. "How could you have kept something like this from me?"

Meanwhile, Lisa nudged Jerry in the ribs. "Pay up. You owe me ten dollars because this is not the usual fish feed you thought it would be. It smells delicious." Lisa lifted the lids. "All my favorite Mexican dishes are here."

Jerry placed his arm around Lisa's shoulder. "You'll have to wait for me to pay. I spent my last paper money on the special treat Brandon just had to have at the burger joint." Jerry placed a fist against his stomach and pushed while he forced a burp. "I'm stuffed, and the burger is sitting heavy."

Lisa gave a look of mock sympathy for his discomfort. "You didn't have to eat. Gail said that she was serving a meal when we arrived."

Jerry forced another burp as he surveyed the feast. "Don't get me wrong; the fish is good food, but not every time we visit." He sampled a chip and some salsa. "Wow, this is good!" Moving around the table to check out the other dishes, Jerry saw Amber sitting in a chair holding a doll and pretending it was her baby. "Hi. Amber. How are you?"

"I'm doing fine. What kind of toy did you buy at the burger place?"

Jerry and Lisa looked at each other with expressions of panic. If Gail found out about them stopping for food before they came, it would hurt her feelings. "Amber, if you can keep a secret about us stopping at the burger place, I will buy you a toy just like the one I bought for Brandon."

"I can keep a secret. What kind of toy is it?"

Gail returned to the dining room with the water before Jerry could tell Amber about the toy, but he held his thumb and index finger to his lips and moved them from side to side as if closing a zipper. Amber smiled and nodded.

This small interaction between Jerry and Amber was noticed by Gail. She chose to ignore it since it was nice to see them bonding. The rest of the family joined them in the dining room. Upon entering, Wade stood beside Gail. He placed his arm around her shoulder to give her a hug and gave her an innocent swat on the behind to remove some dust he claimed was there and then rubbed the spot.

Lisa's jaw dropped as she covered her son's eyes. "Please refrain from such behavior while we are here."

"What did I do?" Wade asked.

"You know very well what you did." Lisa glared at Wade. "There are impressionable children in this house, and we need to protect their innocence."

Wade lifted his hands above his shoulders for all to see and motioned toward the table. "Please help yourself to the food, and don't be shy about it. There's plenty more where that came from."

Instead of the anticipated rush, everyone remained perfectly still. Jason and Amber never moved because they had been told to wait until the company had filled their plates, and the rest of the family were waiting because they were already full.

The lack of movement gave Gail a sinking feeling. She feared that her family was not appreciative of the menu change. "I'm sorry that it's not the usual meal that I prepare, but I thought that you might enjoy a change."

Her father placed his arm around her shoulder. "The food that I sampled behind your back was excellent, and I am going to enjoy eating it later. Right now I'm not that hungry."

"I would like to wait until Dale is here so we can eat together as a family," Jerry said as he lifted Brandon to his knee.

"Dale is coming too?" Gail's mother asked excitedly as she turned to Gail.

Gail smiled. "Dale has an official function to attend before he can be with us." She kept the smile to hide her uncertainty about whether Dale was going to join them. The last conversation with Amanda had not instilled a lot of confidence in Gail.

Gail could tell that once again her mother was annoyed, but at least it seemed like pleasant annoyance at this latest deception. "If Dale is coming to join us, we will all wait for him before we eat!" said her mother.

Although the adults were in agreement about waiting for Dale, Gail knew that Jason and Amber were hungry and wanted to eat. She watched Amber fuss and wondered what was going on in that pretty head. Gail didn't have to wait long for an answer because Amber soon voiced her displeasure at the top of her lungs.

"Just because you thought we were having fish tonight and ate before you came doesn't mean that I should have to wait!" Amber looked at her mother. "Can Jason and I please eat before I starve to death?"

Gail helped Amber dish up some food before she turned and left the room. She was saddened to learn after all these years that her family hated the seafood dishes she thought they loved. By the time Gail returned, everyone was eating, some quite slowly and deliberately, some at a moderate pace, but none as fast as Jason and Amber.

Gail's father put down his fork and walked over to Gail. "Sweetheart, I'm sorry if we hurt your feelings by eating before we came, but it's not because we don't like the food you prepare."

Gail wondered what he could possibly say to convince her otherwise. She remained silent, not sure whether she was doing so to give her father time to spin his yarn to convince her of his sincerity or whether it was a way to avoid saying something that might turn the reunion into a disaster before it even started.

Finally, her father said, "I ate before we came on doctor's orders."

"Doctor's orders?" Gail wondered where this story was leading.

"Yes, doctor's orders. I went to the doctor the other day, and he told me that I'm a little bit diabetic."

"Saying someone is a little bit diabetic is like saying that a woman is a little bit pregnant. You are either diabetic or not diabetic." Gail hoped that the sharpness of her response wasn't as bad as she felt it was, but it must have been because the levity in her father's voice disappeared.

"The doctor said that I must never miss a meal. That is why we stopped for something to eat, not because of your cooking and especially not because of the fish."

Jerry handed Brandon to Lisa and gave Gail a hug. "We are so sorry if we hurt your feelings, but you know what it's like traveling with a hungry child."

Gail looked at him and remembered how as a child Jerry would blame everything on Dale if he thought that he could get away with it. Now she wondered how her brother could even think about blaming this on such a sweet child. But she listened to what Jerry had to say.

"Brandon was hungry and wanted a burger, so we stopped. The food smelled so good that we each had a small burger with Brandon." Jerry paused. "As for me, I enjoy the fish."

Gail wanted to believe them and had no desire to upset the reunion over food. She dried her eyes. "Thank you for being such a wonderful family, and next time I promise not to serve you fish."

While waiting for Dale to arrive, the adults visited, and they all played games. When the phone rang, Gail expected the kids to make a mad dash to answer it. After the third ring she saw that the kids were involved in the games and had no intention of leaving their place at the table. She quickly went to the kitchen to answer the phone. "Hello?"

On the other end of the line, Dale started to laugh. "Sis, you need to learn how to relax and enjoy the moment. You sound stressed."

Gail composed herself and said, "I love you too. So where are you, and when are you going to be here?"

The sound of breaking glass and screaming in the background on Dale's end was muffled by what sounded like Dale placing his hand over the mouthpiece. A moment later, during a brief silence, Dale said, "Something unexpected came up, and I'm going to be busy for a while longer tonight." There were more sounds of unhappy screaming and breaking glass. "I gotta go, sis. I'll be at your house first thing in the morning. I promise."

Gail wished that Dale could be with them. "Are you sure that being here tonight is out of the question?"

Glass broke in the background again. It sounded as if a vase had broken next to Dale's head. "I'm positive, sis. This is a big deal. I'll see you in the morning."

Gail was disappointed that Dale was going to miss the first night of the reunion, but she was also aware that his was an important job that at times knew no set working hours. "I'm sorry you can't be here. I will tell the others you will be here when you can."

Before she had finished speaking, there was a beep on the line; she had another call. She quickly said good-bye to Dale.

"Hello?"

"Hello." The voice on the other end sounded friendly enough, but the man seemed uncertain about how to proceed. "Is this Gail Rollins? Formerly known as Gail Evers?"

Gail's interest was piqued by these two seemingly innocent, yet awkward questions. "Yes, it is." Gail waited for the man to continue.

"You don't know me, but I wish to speak with you."

"Okay." Gail said cautiously as she began to wonder if she should hang up. "What can I do for you?"

"Do you mind if I ask when your birthday is?"

"Excuse me?"

Gail's reaction caused the man to speak softly, almost apologetic. "Please let me ask that differently. If I told you a date, would you confirm that it is your birthday?"

"Maybe," Gail listened to the man tell her the date. "Yes, that is my birthday." There were sounds of excitement in the background after she answered, and it intrigued her. As she listened intently to the sounds, the man surprised her with his next question.

"Were you adopted?"

"Excuse me - why would you ask me that?" Gail asked, suddenly concerned where this conversation was leading. "So who are you?"

The man spoke softly. "Based on the information we have been able to obtain, there is a good chance that you are the girl my wife gave up for adoption, and she would like to meet with you. That is, if you would like to meet with her."

Gail was speechless as she came to the realization that this man knew her biological mother, and the hair bristled on the back of her neck. Gail felt a shortness of breath. Was it possible that after all these years she would finally meet the lady who had given her life? Years of pent-up emotion were coming to the surface as she struggled to maintain her composure. Was it possible that after all this time this was actually happening?

The man continued, "We don't want to disrupt your life or make things difficult for you. So now that you know that your birth mother would like to meet with you, the question is, do you want to meet with her?"

"Yes, I would love to meet her." Saying those words brought a release of emotion that Gail felt was years overdue. It took all she had to stay in control.

"Good. We will be in town on Tuesday night and were hoping that you could meet us in the food court at the mall."

"What time?" Gail asked, as she reached for a pen.

"What works best for you?"

When the meeting time had been decided, they finished speaking, and the man hung up the phone. Gail sat motionless, with the receiver still to her ear. Tears flowed freely as she placed the receiver onto the cradle and reached for a tissue. When the box on the telephone desk was empty, Gail slipped quietly down the hallway for more tissues.

In the bathroom Gail looked at her reflection. The red eyes and streaked mascara made it quite obvious that she had been crying. She slipped away to her room to repair her makeup and then waited a few more minutes to compose herself before joining the family. Gail wanted to shout her good news from the rooftop and tell anyone who would listen, but she didn't because she wanted to share the news with Wade first. Yet the prospect of sharing the news made her hesitate. She wondered, what would Wade say about her planning the meeting during the reunion? She had been very explicit that nothing was to be scheduled this week that would take away from the reunion.

"What took you so long? It's your turn," Amber asked as Gail returned to the room. Amber handed Gail her cards.

Wade looked closely at Gail's face, as if he could see that something had happened. "Who was on the phone?"

"Dale."

"When is he coming?" Wade asked.

"He will be unable to join us tonight. Something came up."

"Dale usually makes people cry by showing up, not by staying away," said Jerry. A sharp jab to the ribs by Lisa reminded him that his remark was not appropriate.

Gail rejoined the group and soon sensed that Amber was becoming bored with the slow speed of the game, which she didn't understand, when she began to ask questions about the strangest things. Gail answered the questions as quickly and quietly as she could and tried to distract Amber in hopes of preventing the next question from being asked. For the family members who knew how difficult this was, not knowing what question was coming next, there was nervous anticipation with a dash of dread. Amber sat silently for a few more minutes and then asked, "Mommy, why did you greet people at the door tonight with a hug and a kiss?"

It seemed like an innocent enough question, but Gail found herself hesitating to respond as she quickly thought of all the possible wrong answers to avoid. During the hesitation, her mother answered for her. "When people greet each other with a hug and a kiss, it's their way of showing that they care for each other a great deal. When your mother greeted us with a hug and kiss, it was to say that she loves us and is happy to welcome us to your home." The answer seemed to do the trick because Amber remained silent and turned her attention back to the game.

A few turns had passed when Amber asked another question. "Mommy, does it mean that Jason loves Vicki because he gave her a hug and a kiss at the front door, even though she was leaving and not coming into the house?"

The room went silent, and Gail felt sorry for Jason. All eyes turned to Jason, who by this time was glowing bright red and staring at his sister in disbelief. The adults started to snicker. Jason rushed to his room.

Amber tugged on Gail's sleeve. "Why did Jason leave before the game was over?"

Eventually, the family retired to their rooms for the evening. On her way to bed, Gail checked in on Jason to see if he was going to survive the embarrassment caused by his sister. "You okay?"

Jason pressed pause on the video game he was playing and turned to Gail. "I'll live. It's my own fault for not making sure that Amber, the walking news service, was away from the door when I said good-bye to Vicki."

After a few minutes of calm, reassuring conversation, Gail was able to leave Jason in a much better mood, especially after they shared a laugh about how those who didn't know Amber as well as they did could be in for an interesting visit.

Amber was already in her pajamas and ready for bed when Gail arrived and closed the bedroom door before kneeling down with Amber for her evening prayers. Gail enjoyed listening to Amber's prayers since this gave her an opportunity to know what was going on inside of that pretty little head. Tonight was no exception.

Amber started her prayer. "Dear Heavenly Father, please bless Uncle Dale that his work will let him be with the family so that Mommy can be happy and not cry again if he calls."

Gail was touched that Amber was so sensitive to the feelings of others and felt pride enter her heart at how wonderful this little girl was. Gail's heart melted, and tears ran down her face as she continued listening.

"Please bless Mommy that she will find Lexie so that the missing puppy can be returned to the dog family."

Gail heard the rest of the prayer but didn't really listen. Her own thoughts went back to those days in the hospital with the lonely, frightened little girl who needed a friend. Amber finished her prayer with a big "Amen." She jumped to her feet and gave Gail a big hug and kiss. "I love you, Mommy!"

"I love you too, sweetheart!" Gail said as she tucked Amber into bed and kissed her forehead.

Gail was in a quiet, thoughtful mood when she arrived at her own bedroom, quiet enough that her arrival was met with a curious question.

"Are you still disappointed that Dale was unable to join us tonight?" Wade gently wiped a tear from below her right eye.

"What makes you think that I'm still disappointed?"

Wade rubbed his fingertips together. "These tears are what make me think you're still disappointed." Wade pulled Gail close. After a short embrace he began to massage the back of her neck and shoulders.

Gail remained motionless and enjoyed the moment as Wade's strong hands and fingers found and relaxed the muscle knots that had taken up residence in her shoulders. "The tears in my eyes are not because of Dale."

"They're not?" Wade's massage slowed. "If the tears are not because of Dale, then what has your waterworks leaking?"

Gail dropped her head forward and gave a few directions regarding where Wade should massage next. "They were from listening to Amber's prayer before I tucked her in for the night." Gail put her arms around Wade. "She prayed for Uncle Dale to arrive so that I could be happy and not cry again should he call."

Wade was about to point out how that meant the tears were because of Dale but thought better of it. "That was thoughtful. But I don't think that deserved any more tears. Dale promised to be here in the morning."

"You're right. It's what she said next that brought the tears." Gail felt embarrassed by the unrelenting tears as she once again wiped her eyes. "Amber is concerned about the missing puppy from the dog family ornament you bought when I was in the hospital pregnant with Jason."

"Why would she be concerned about that?"

"Amber wants the puppy back to make the dog family whole again."

Wade sighed. "You're thinking about Lexie again, aren't you?"

Gail knew that Wade didn't want the thoughts of Lexie to affect another Christmas season. "Maybe a little bit."

A hint of frustration was present in Wade's voice as he said, "Sweetheart, I realize that your time in the hospital was emotional for a number of reasons." His voice softened. "You need to let go. She is someone else's daughter, and you must accept that there is nothing more that you can do for her."

"I do know that." Gail reached for a dry tissue. "The part I can't forget is my promise to be there for her, and then I wasn't."

The room was silent except for Wade's deliberate breathing until he spoke. "You were fortunate enough to be her friend when she desperately needed one. You were like a mother to her and consoled her when she was alone and frightened." Wade took a deep breath. "You did all that you could, but now she is with her family."

"I know you're right, but I just can't help it."

Wade took Gail in his arms and spoke gently in her ear. "I love how you would try to save every child from being alone and experiencing pain if you could. Unfortunately, you can only look out for and protect those close to you, and you are doing a wonderful job with our children."

"Thank you," Gail said as she gave him a kiss. "I feel bad that Amber will have to deal with the disappointment of the missing puppy until she outgrows the notion of finding Lexie." Gail pulled back the sheets and climbed into bed. She fluffed the pillow behind her back, took a book from the nightstand, and opened it as if to read but then closed the pages and laid the book down. She still had to share her news with Wade. "How am I going to tell my mother about the phone call I received tonight?" she said quietly.

The look on Wade's face when he rolled toward her made Gail laugh. "We all know the story about your call from Dale, so what more is there to tell your mother?" Wade folded the pillow under his head for support.

Gail fidgeted with the corner of her book. "There's a lot more to tell her."

"Was there a surprise about the call that you kept from us?" He paused briefly. "Let me guess—your brother is getting married tonight and wants to surprise us with an introduction to his new bride tomorrow!"

Gail laughed. "Don't be silly. Even I couldn't keep a secret like that."

"Then what do you need to tell your mother?"

Gail stared straight ahead. "There was a second phone call tonight."

"The phone only rang once." Wade tried to stifle a yawn. "It rang only once."

Gail corrected him. "There were two calls. The phone never rang twice because of call waiting." She swallowed hard and reached for a tissue.

"Who was the second caller?" Wade propped his head with his pillow again.

Tears began to run down her face as once again emotions surfaced. "I don't know his name. He never told me."

"What did the man say?" Wade asked as he watched Gail struggle for control.

Gail laughed as she looked at him through her tears. "The man asked when my birthday was."

Wade was curious about Gail's behavior. "Why would a man phone to ask about your birthday, and why are you acting this way?"

Gail stared at Wade with the look she gave when she felt that he should know the answer before she had to tell him. "My birthday is on the information release form that I filled out. The one that would help a child given up for adoption find her birth mother or help the birth mother find the child."

Wade remained silent a few moments, inwardly hoping that this meant what he thought it meant. "So what did the man want?"

She took a deep breath while she struggled to open the soggy tissue that was now rolled into a tight ball. "The man on the phone is married to my birth mother, and wanted to set up a meeting with me, and his wife – my birth mother."

"That's wonderful!" Wade wrapped his arms around her and kissed her. He could only imagine the emotions she was feeling. "What did you tell him?"

Gail looked at Wade through her tears. "I told him yes."

"Perfect!" He kissed her again. "When is the meeting?"

Gail was excited and nervous. "The meeting is set for Tuesday night."

"This Tuesday night?" Wade paused. "During the family reunion?"

"Yes, this Tuesday." Gail knew what point Wade was going to make.

"During the family reunion, when no other plans were to be made?" Wade laughed.

Some days, she hated it when Wade was right. It was her rule, and she had made plans that would take her away from family. She thought about the situation. "There are exceptions to every rule if you think about it. I feel good about this exception because being away from family to be with family is still being with family."

Wade gave a yawn that could have set a world record for length. "So if I'm right, the question is whether you are going to inform your mother of your plans to ditch her, to be with your other mother during this festival of family bonding, or simply let it happen without her knowledge."

Hearing the situation stated like that gave Gail reason to pause. Had she set the meeting for after the reunion, there would be no issue, but if she put off the meeting, it might never happen. "What am I to do?"

They talked about the issue well into the early morning hours.

"So we are agreed that you should tell your mother about the meeting," Wade finally said.

"Yes."

"We are also aware that there is no right time to share the news with your mother because of all the family who are unaware of the situation." Wade laid his pillow flat and reached for the light switch.

"Right. I do not wish this meeting to be the center of attention. The family is the main focus." The lights went out. "You will have to create a diversion so Mother and I can have a moment to talk." Gail wondered how much of her final request Wade had heard over his deep breathing.

Chapter Five

BREAKFAST SHOULD HAVE BEEN quick and simple according to Gail's master plan. Unfortunately, she had made the mistake of providing more than one choice of cold cereal for the younger children. Amber was easy to serve since she always wanted the same sugar-coated wheat puffs. Brandon, on the other hand, was proving to be more difficult. He would decide on a cereal only to change his mind once the milk had been added. Gail obliged her young nephew for the first couple of changes but then insisted that he make up his mind. She soon learned that the more she insisted, the more stubborn he became. The more stubborn he became, the more Gail's frustration grew, to where she wondered where his parents were.

Jerry finally made an appearance. "Good morning, sis."

"Good morning, Jerry. Did you sleep well?"

"I slept great." He stretched his hands above his head. "Sorry about last night and for making you feel bad about the fish and seafood dishes you like to serve."

"That's okay. I just thought that everyone looked forward to it. Boy, was I wrong."

"It's our fault for not telling you. We were wrong to keep leading you on." Jerry watched the kids at the table. "So how is breakfast going?"

"Lousy!"

"Why is it going lousy?"

Gail watched Brandon push away another bowl. "Brandon is undecided about what he wants for breakfast, and we are wasting a lot of food."

Jerry tried to feed Brandon a spoonful of cereal only to have the spoon pushed away and the cereal fall to the table. "He is a fussy eater." He tried to land the food in Brandon's mouth a second time with the same level of success. "Lisa is the one who knows how to reason with him and make him eat."

Gail was still tired from her lack of sleep and was losing her patience with how difficult this simple breakfast had become. "So where is Lisa?"

Jerry popped some cereal into his mouth. "She is still in bed and will be there for a while longer."

"Is she not feeling well?"

"To get Lisa to the reunion, I told her to treat it like a vacation. Unfortunately, I didn't think that she would take a vacation from everything, including her parental duties. With so much family around to watch over Brandon, she informed me that she is going to sleep in and enjoy herself."

Any concern Gail might have had for Lisa's well-being left as quickly as it had arrived and was replaced by contempt. Before Gail could respond and possibly say something inappropriate, Brandon started to fuss and complain.

"I don't want orange juice. I want grape!"

Jerry sighed. "He will drink nothing but grape juice." Jerry went to the refrigerator and located the bottle of concentrate and mixed a pitcher of juice. "Brandon likes everything grape, from his juice in the morning to the gum he chews. The boy is a grapeaholic."

Gail left Jerry to deal with his son and went to make sure there was an adequate supply of towels and toiletries on hand for everyone. She returned and was shocked to find the table covered with every cereal bowl from the cupboard, each one filled with a small portion of cereal and milk. Some bowls even had cereal with grape drink instead of milk. At first she thought they were all from Jerry's attempts to find the perfect cereal for his son. A closer examination of the scene revealed that Amber was now playing the game and had a different bowl as well.

Gail took a deep breath—several, in fact—to remain calm and resist the urge to take Brandon over her knee for being such a spoiled brat. She even found herself fantasizing about putting her brother over her knee for allowing such a cute child to become the bratty monster he was showing himself to be.

The collection of partially filled cereal bowls caught everyone's attention as the family entered the kitchen. The children's grandma was the one to make the biggest fuss over it. "Tomorrow I am going to cook a special breakfast for everyone—special because I am going to take orders and cook to satisfy every request."

"You don't have to do that, Mom." Gail gave her a hug. "Cold cereal will be just fine. I never intended for you to wait on everyone hand and foot." Gail watched as her mother looked at the children and then at all the bowls.

"These children obviously want something other than cold cereal, or they would have used only one bowl each and been done eating by now. They need a proper breakfast."

Gail gathered the bowls and placed them in the sink. The nearest she could figure was that a gallon of milk and two boxes of cereal went down the drain. She listened as her mother asked what each child wanted for breakfast.

"Amber, what would you like Grandma to make you for breakfast tomorrow?"

Amber sat up straight and requested her favorite snack. "I want cinnamon toast nontoastered, with the crusts off, folded in half and cut to my little size."

The momentary look of confusion on Gail's mother's face was priceless, and Gail thought that it would be wiser to talk about the new breakfast plan later.

Her attention turned from breakfast planning to the sight of Jason entering the kitchen. Standing in the doorway was a very well-dressed young man in his finest clothes, a far cry from the outrageous outfit he had chosen the night before.

Brandon and Amber finished with breakfast, and Jason moved out of their way to let them pass. Jason breathed a sigh of relief when the children were gone, and his clothes were still clean and free from stains.

In the other room Amber and Brandon started to squeal with excitement about the big black car in front of the house. Everyone except Jason left the kitchen to greet Dale. Jason stayed behind to finish breakfast before Vicki arrived.

Dale entered the kitchen and greeted Jason. He stepped back and gave a low whistle along with an approving nod. "Nice clothes. Are you modeling them for your mother, or do you have a date?"

Jason smiled. "I'm going to a dance recital."

"Oh, so you have a date."

Jason sighed. "Yes, I have a date."

"Lucky girl." Dale gave Jason a high five and then turned his attention to the refrigerator. "So what was for breakfast?"

Gail entered the kitchen. "Cold cereal—sugar-coated wheat or corn puffs."

"Are you serious?" He rummaged through the fridge and emerged with a bowl of hot peppers. "I never would have imagined that my sister would allow any of these little guys into her house." Dale peeled back the wrapper covering the bowl. "Most people think that the only hot pepper that exists is the jalapeño, which is really too bad since they are missing out on the finer things of life."

"Be careful with those!" Jason placed his hand over the bowl to prevent Dale from grabbing a pepper. "Vicki warned us that they should only be used as a table decoration."

With a wry smile Dale popped two of the peppers into his mouth and chewed a few times before swallowing. "I'm sure that Vicki means well when she warns people about peppers. As you can see, they are about as hot as a gumdrop." Dale popped another pepper into his mouth and showed definite signs of enjoyment. "All the way to town, my mouth was watering for some of these little fellas. There were supposed to be some at the wedding I came to attend." He gave a thoughtful pause. "Unfortunately, the bride called the wedding off at the last moment and sent the groom packing."

Gail grinned at the realization that her food had come from the same wedding. "Did she send the bridesmaids packing as well?"

Dale stopped and looked at Gail. "You know about what happened?"

Gail smiled. "The caterer told me when he offered me a feast of authentic Mexican food that he no longer had a place to serve. "He said that the groom had invited all the beautiful young bridesmaids to his room for a party without the bride's knowledge."

Dale raised an eyebrow as he looked at Gail. "How do you know he did this without her knowledge?"

Gail laughed. "Had she known, she might have had a weapon when she found them."

Dale winced. "You're probably right." He ate another pepper and then offered one to Jason.

Jason started to reach out. He hesitated and then pulled his hand away. "Vicki says these are dangerous."

"What does she know?" Dale scoffed as he ate another of the allegedly dangerous peppers to show how safe they were. "You don't know what you are missing."

Numerous past practical jokes had made trusting his uncle difficult for Jason. Vicki had been serious when she warned about the peppers. Yet he had just seen Dale act as if he had eaten a gumdrop.

Jason reached for a pepper and popped it into his mouth. He chewed twice and swallowed and seemed to be perfectly fine—until the burning sensation began to grow. Jason was in obvious discomfort when he gasped and reached for his throat. He started to pant and wave his hand in front of his mouth. Looking frantic, he pushed past Dale to the sink, turned on the tap, cupped his hands under the stream of cold water, and tried to gulp the refreshing liquid. Not finding relief, Jason turned his head and let the water run directly into his open mouth.

Gail offered Jason some bread and pulled a carton of milk from the refrigerator. Her concern for Jason was greater than the contempt she felt for Dale, who was doubled over in uncontrollable fits of laughter that brought tears to his eyes.

Meanwhile, the doorbell rang, and a few moments later, Amber brought Vicki to see Jason. Vicki saw the open bowl of peppers in Dale's hand and Jason in distress being tended to by his mother. She rushed to Jason's side and placed a tablet in his mouth. "Chew this!"

In a few moments Jason found relief. "Thank you."

"You're welcome," Vicki said, rubbing Jason's shoulder.

Jason wiped droplets of water from his face and touched the front of his wet jacket as he looked at Dale. "How can you eat these things?"

Dale was still amused by the success of his latest practical joke. "I have eaten a lot of spicy foods, and the inside of my mouth is not very sensitive anymore." Dale wiped his eyes. "I still owed you for the stunt you pulled the last time I was here."

Jason was about to respond but was stopped by Vicki. "You should go change into some dry clothes."

They walked down the hallway and stopped when Jason saw his reflection in the full-length mirror at the end of the hallway. The reflection was not that of a well-groomed young man ready to spend the day with a wonderful young lady. What he saw was a drowned rat, his hair a mess and his clothes dripping wet, standing beside the most beautiful girl in the world. He groaned. "Here stand beauty and the beast."

"Not so! You are a little wet. The beast is still in the kitchen." Vicki took Jason by the hand. "Do you still want to go to my recital?"

Jason was slow to respond to Vicki's question because he was distracted by the payback plans already coming to mind.

"If you don't want to go, I will understand. Just let me know because my friend Alexis is in the car, and we have to go."

Payback was going to be sweet, but not at the cost of missing a day with Vicki. "I'm going to change my clothes, and then we will go to the recital." Jason turned and took the stairs two at a time.

Vicki returned to the kitchen, where Dale was letting out yet another loud laugh. The laugh was cut short when Vicki stood face-to-face with Dale. There was no mistaking the fire in her eyes. "What were you thinking?"

Dale's eyes met Vicki's. "It was a joke."

Vicki let Dale know what she thought about the juvenile prank and proceeded to give Dale a brief but thorough lesson on the dangers of certain foods. There was a very tangible tension in the air. None of the adults seemed willing to say anything for fear of making a bad situation worse.

Amber broke the silence. "Mommy, do people talk that way when someone they love has been hurt?"

Gail was at a loss for words in response to the question and wanted to avoid further embarrassing a now blushing Vicki. "Uncle Dale was a bad boy, and Vicki just told him how bad he was before Mommy could tell him."

The answer must have worked because Amber had no further questions before she ran off to play.

Dale had a changed demeanor when Jason returned. "Nice suit—almost as nice as your other one."

Jason was silent for a moment. This was the time when Dale would usually gloat over his latest success, yet something was different. "Thank you ... I think."

Vicki moved across the room until she was standing next to Jason. Her expression showed that she was not happy with Dale's feeble attempt at making peace. He extended his hand toward Jason. "I am sorry for tricking you into eating those peppers. It was wrong, and I know that now."

Jason reluctantly accepted Dale's apology and left the kitchen with Vicki. "What happened while I was upstairs changing my clothes?"

Vicki wrapped her arm around his and smiled.

Chapter Six

LAUGHTER COMING FROM THE family was the sound Gail had hoped to hear during the reunion. She should have been happy, but right now she was disappointed to be cleaning the kitchen alone while the family was gathered in the living room, listening to Dale tell his tales. When the final bowl was placed in the cupboard and the countertops were wiped down, Gail joined the family.

Amber and Brandon were playing away from the main group while the adults were gathered close to Dale—everyone except for Lisa, who was still missing in action. Gail found a place next to Wade and listened to the tales and watched her family enjoying themselves.

Lisa joined the family a short while later, looking refreshed with her hair still wet and tousled. She sat next to Jerry and finished a piece of toast. She washed it down with a tall glass of milk and placed the empty glass on the new end table. Not wanting to make a scene and destroy the mood, Gail took a deep breath and resisted the urge to comment or jump up and remove the offending glass.

Amber came over and stared at Lisa. "Mommy says we are not to eat in this room. I'll take your empty glass to the kitchen this time." Gail watched as Amber left and then returned to continue playing with Brandon, all without so much as a thank-you from Lisa.

Lisa appeared bored and interrupted Dale. "So what was so important last night that it kept you from gracing us with your presence?"

"I already told that story over breakfast, but I would be happy to tell it to you later."

The response was unsatisfactory to Lisa, and she made it apparent that she was not going to be denied. "Well, I just ate breakfast and never heard the story!"

Dale drew a deep breath and sighed as he once again described in great detail the events of the day before.

Lisa showed impatience at how slowly the story was being told. "So what happened to upset the bride?"

Dale politely continued his story as the narrative it was intended to be.

"At this rate I will be preparing for my son's wedding before you finish telling the story!"

The look Dale gave Lisa was not as polite and dignified as the first time, but his training as a diplomat helped him remain calm. He cleared his throat and then squared his shoulders and sat facing Lisa. "To make a long story short … the bride had entered the room to find the groom entertaining the bridesmaids."

"So what was so wrong with him entertaining the girls?"

Dale gave a big sigh as he looked over at his brother, who could do nothing more than smile and shrug. Dale then turned back to Lisa. "There was nothing wrong if you think it normal to be entertaining all of the girls except for the bride in his bedroom, the night before his wedding."

The room was silent except for the small gasp that escaped Lisa's lips as she comprehended what had happened. Her wide eyes narrowed. "How could you be so inconsiderate and tell a story like that in front of these impressionable children?"

"You insisted that I tell you the story right now. So I did."

The more Dale smiled, the angrier Lisa's scowl became. Gail also noticed how quiet the rest of the family was becoming and remembered how the last reunion had gone bad. "Dale did say that he would rather tell you the story at another time."

Lisa's hands clenched into fists as she stood and stormed from the room without saying another word.

Amber came over to Gail. "Mommy, did Uncle Dale do something wrong, and because Aunt Lisa loves him so much, she scolded him before you could?"

The family that remained began to laugh uncontrollably.

Gail had a sinking feeling. The laughter from her family that she had heard earlier was what she had hoped for. But this time she worried that the laughter might be misunderstood by Lisa since she hadn't heard Amber's question.

Amber, meanwhile, had found a new shadow. Brandon followed her every move and was never more than a few feet away from her. He even waited for her outside the bathroom. In a desperate attempt to lose Brandon, Amber took him to her room and showed him her fish tank with all of the colorful fish swimming around. It seemed to work—Brandon was mesmerized by the fish, and he didn't move from his position in front of the tank when Amber left the room.

Later, Lisa came looking for Brandon. "Amber, have you seen Brandon?"

"He was looking at the fish in my room."

Amber and Lisa entered Amber's room, and Brandon was still watching the fish. Only now there was a chair beside the tank and an empty bottle of grape drink mix in the center of a large purple stain on the plush white carpet.

Lisa rushed over and lightly touched the soggy purple stain as she picked up the bottle. "Amber, where does your mother keep the carpet cleaner?"

Amber ran from the room, crying in a shrill voice, "Mommy!"

In no time she returned with Gail in tow. When they entered the room, Gail's attention was immediately drawn to the large purple stain. Lisa was trying to soak up the spilled grape concentrate with one of the new white towels from the bathroom.

Before Gail could comment about the towel, her attention was quickly diverted by a woeful scream from Amber. Gail looked over and saw Amber in tears, her little fingers pressing against the glass, pointing as one of her favorite fish rolled over and stayed upside down. The once crystal clear water of the fish tank was now clouded by a swirling mist of purple drink mix as it circulated from the top of the tank to the bottom. The normally active fish that would dart to the surface and attack the tiniest of air bubbles were now having difficulty breathing and staying right side up, let alone swimming.

Gail ignored Lisa and the stain as she lifted Brandon from directly in front of the tank and sat him on the chair he had used to pour his drink mix in with the fish. Gail then sat Amber on the bed—close enough that Amber could see what was happening, but with enough distance that Gail could shield her actions from Amber. Gail removed the large cover from the tank and began to scoop the tiny fish out of the clouded water with the small net.

Aware that Amber was watching her every move, Gail was careful to remove the living fish and place them in the container of freshwater on the stand beside the tank. As each of the dead fish was placed in a second container, the tears began to fall freely down Amber's face.

Gail looked at Brandon and between Amber's screams and sobs asked, "Why did you do it?"

With a large smile Brandon replied, "The fish looked thirsty, so I gave them something to drink."

As Gail tried to understand the response, another fish stopped moving in the freshwater container, and Amber made it known to all with her screams.

Lisa began defending the actions of her son. "He is only a little boy and didn't know any better."

With the sobbing and wailing of Amber in one ear and the illogical excuses and rationalizations from Lisa in the other, Gail politely asked Lisa to remove Brandon from the room and keep an eye on him.

It was obvious that Lisa was offended. She turned her head sharply to one side, raised her nose in the air, and snorted as she took Brandon by the hand and stormed out of the room. Brandon, meanwhile, was fighting his mother's grip every step of the way, screaming at the top of his lungs about wanting to stay with the fish.

With all of the live fish now in the smaller container, Gail looked at the tank with the swirling patterns of purple coming from the filters and pushed her sleeves up past the elbow. Setting up the tank siphon, she began the task of changing the water. Amber was at her mother's side, trying to help where she could, but she was more of a hindrance than a help. As another fish rolled over, Amber started to cry and began saying nasty things about her cousin.

Gail immediately stopped what she was doing and took the opportunity to teach Amber a life lesson. She sat down with her daughter in the middle of the mess and told her that sometimes bad things happen that were intended to be nice. She explained that Brandon had thought he was doing something nice for the fish when he gave them his grape drink. Gail made a point of telling Amber repeatedly that Brandon hadn't meant to hurt the fish. Amber soon bombarded Gail with the expected storm of questions that came anytime an explanation was required. Eventually, all of the questions were answered, and Gail was feeling almost hypocritical because her answers to Amber were inconsistent with the desires of her own heart regarding how to deal with the situation.

Mother and daughter then returned to the task at hand. Gail promised to replace each fish that had died with two others if Amber would relax and not mention what had happened to the fish again. Amber promised, and soon the water in the tank was changed. The remaining fish were starting to move about the smaller container with some energy, which helped to calm Amber, but she was still upset by the small number of fish that had survived.

Eventually, Gail was able to return the surviving fish to the friendly confines of the large tank. Brandon wanted to come see the fish again but found Amber closing the door in his face and holding it closed while her young cousin cried loudly on the other side.

Gail's numerous attempts to remove the horrid purple stain from the carpet had failed, and the stain was as bright as ever. Wanting to avoid another scene with Lisa over the whole situation, Gail covered the stain with a smaller rug and made a mental note to call the carpet cleaners after the holiday.

Seeing Amber holding the doorknob tightly and keeping the door shut brought a smile to Gail's lips. Her daughter had a mind of her own and knew what she wanted. But Brandon's vocal complaints concerned Gail because they had been going on far too long without Lisa stepping in to calm her son.

Gail knelt down beside Amber. "I think that it would be okay for Brandon to come in and watch the fish because he isn't going to hurt them anymore."

"No!" Amber protested.

Gail took Amber in her arms. "Can Brandon please come into your room to watch the fish?"

"No!"

Not wanting to sound as if she was begging, Gail spoke with Amber calmly and explained that Brandon needed a second chance. Eventually, Amber relented and opened the door to let Brandon in.

After a few minutes, Gail took Amber and Brandon down to the kitchen with her for a small snack. Amber closed the bedroom door firmly behind them. Once in the kitchen, Gail gave the children a snack of cheese and crackers and then sent them off to play.

Before she started to prepare the evening meal, Gail was distracted by the sound of her dog yelping and growling like it did when Jason teased it. "Now what is going on?" Gail muttered as she heard the unmistakable sound of Brandon crying. Her dog came running into the kitchen and stood behind her legs. Gail noticed a large wad of grape gum in the short white fur as she picked up the dog.

Brandon came in crying. "The doggy stole my gum!"

Gail could see the humor in the situation but was frustrated. Lisa, the missing-in-action mother, never came to see what was happening with Brandon. Gail saw Amber watching her every move and knew that if she acted badly in response to the situation, Amber would have a million questions, and her prior explanations about how to act would be wasted.

Taking a deep breath, Gail placed the dog on the floor and took Brandon in her arms to calm him. "What happened?"

He was still upset and cried, "The dog stole my gum when I tried to give him a kiss."

Gail smiled. "You go ask your mom for some more gum." She took the dog and marched quickly from the room without saying another word, picking at the wad of purple gum and shaking her head as she walked. On the way to clean the dog, she walked past Lisa sitting on the couch, totally oblivious to anything going on around her. It seemed that Lisa was expecting a vacation from all responsibilities of motherhood because of the abundance of unpaid babysitters in the house.

The little dog complained bitterly during the removal of gum from his fur, even taking a nip at Gail from time to time to show his displeasure. Eventually, Gail got out all of the gum and was available to join the rest of the family, who now it seemed were not to be found. So far the activities of her day had been completely different than what she had planned. She had expected to spend her time speaking with her mother and visiting with family, not cleaning up after her nephew while his mother watched TV.

While Gail was cleaning the fish tank, her parents had taken the opportunity to drive home, to retrieve the gifts they would have brought with them had they been told the whole family was going to be at Gail's for Christmas, and they still hadn't returned. Now would have been the perfect opportunity to talk with her mother, but it would have to wait until later; the only question was how much later. Jason was who knows where, doing who knows what with Vicki and her friend, considering the recital had been over for at least five hours. Wade had taken Jerry and Dale to do some last-minute shopping as part of the plan to give Gail time to speak with her parents. It had seemed like a good plan until her parents' decision to drive home had left Gail with nothing more to do than watch over the kingdom.

Gail went to the kitchen to prepare the evening meal. With no one there except Lisa and the children and with no idea how late people would be returning, she reached for the numerous bowls of Mexican food. The sight of the bowl of peppers brought a smile to her face as she remembered the distress Dale had caused Jason by conning him into eating one pepper. The smile had less to do with the actual incident than with how Vicki had taken Dale to task until he apologized. An apology was something the family very seldom heard from Dale because to him it seemed that everything he said and did was always right.

Gail felt bad setting the table with the same meal two nights in a row but was willing to live with it considering how much Mexican food was still left. It was almost time to leave for Amber's program, and the children needed to eat. "Amber, Brandon!" she called. Gail hesitated as she considered the prospect of feeding her nephew by herself. "Lisa … it's time to eat."

Since she had been snacking all day, the refried beans were looking less appealing with every bite. Amber and Brandon only picked at their food before they left the kitchen, and Gail couldn't blame them. After the dishes had been cleared away and washed, Gail went to find Amber to get her dressed for the program. Finding Amber was easy since after this morning's episode, she had spent her day keeping

Brandon from killing any more fish. Amber would only allow him to come up to, but not over, the piece of tape she had placed on the floor in front of the tank.

Gail reached Amber's room and said, "Brandon, your mother wants you."

With Brandon out of the way, it was girl time. Soon Amber had been transformed from a lovely little girl into a beautiful angel. Her hair was done to perfection, with every strand in its proper place. The costume, with wings and halo, was without a single wrinkle and seemed to shine. Now that the star of the show was ready, Gail wondered whether the family would return in time to watch the program—or for that matter get Amber to the church on time.

The front door opened and then closed with a resounding thud, followed closely by the energetic thump of feet taking the stairs two at a time.

"How was your day with Vicki?" Gail asked. She stepped into the hallway to slow him down. "Was it a good recital?"

Jason thought for a moment. "The recital was all right, I guess."

"How did Vicki do?"

Jason tried to work his way past Gail. "Mom, it was dancing. The mall afterward was a lot more fun."

"You went to the mall?"

Unable to get past his mother, Jason wrapped his arms around her. "Love you, Mom," he said, as if that was the magic phrase to make her move. When she didn't let him past, he said, "Could you please move so I can change my clothes? I have places to be."

Gail held her ground. "The only place that you need to be is with family. Remember, I told you that during the reunion, family comes first." She watched Jason's shoulders slump. "Are the plans with Vicki?"

"No. She has plans to go caroling around their neighborhood with friends tonight. Charles and the guys want me to go out with them."

Gail thought for a moment. "Charles is supposed to be at the program with his family, just like you are supposed to be with us tonight. I can't let you go."

He tried to plead his case but never found the right words to convince his mother. Jason finally lowered his head. "You're right. I should be with family."

"That's better. Now hurry up and change for Amber's program."

Jason opened his bedroom door just far enough to enter the room. Before the door closed behind him, he muttered, "Besides, I need to stay close to Uncle Dale so I can get even for what he did to me this morning."

Gail corrected him. "You need to be with family because they are family, and you need to spend time with them, not to plan how to get even with them."

The side door from the garage opened, and Gail heard the rustling of packages mixed with the sounds of the men's voices. She waited until she could see them at the bottom of the steps and then said, "We need to leave shortly for the program." It was at that moment Gail noticed that Dale wasn't with them. "Where's Dale?" Gail stooped down to gain a better view. "Is he still in the garage bringing in his gifts?"

Jerry looked to Wade, who said, "We dropped Dale off at the embassy. He told us to tell you how sorry he was for stepping out on you, but he will rejoin the family in the morning."

Gail wondered whether Dale had experienced enough family time and was using work as an escape. "Is that all he said?"

Wade smiled. "Dale made one other statement that I found quite interesting."

"What was it?"

"He said that he is so glad to have you for a sister and that you don't take no for an answer when it comes to keeping the family together." Wade chuckled. "He also said that he is looking forward to seeing what adventures in family bonding the rest of the reunion will bring."

Gail didn't know what to make of the final comment but didn't have time to dwell on the intent. Time was running out to make it to the program.

Her parents pulled up in front of the house just as everyone was leaving. Gail noticed that Jason was nowhere to be found. She returned to find him still in his room, lying on the bed.

"I'm not feeling well," he said. "You should just leave me home."

Gail suspected that once they left, his friends would stop by to pick him up. Soon a sober-looking Jason was in the backseat of the van. He had to be in the back since Amber took up the entire second row to keep her costume and hair from becoming mussed.

Partway to the church, Amber complained that Jason was trying to kill her when a nasty smell drifted from the back of the van.

"I'm sorry, but Mom made me come, even after I told her I wasn't feeling well."

As each hot pepper–based assault to the sense of smell was launched, the windows were rolled down. At first the family rolled down the windows just a crack. As the air quality worsened, the windows were rolled down even farther, and heads poked outside of the van for breaths of cool, crisp fresh air.

When they finally arrived at the church, the family looked as if there had been a tornado inside the van. Amber's previously well-combed hair was a mess. The halo that had sat so squarely above her head was now bent and resting on Amber's left shoulder. Jason wasn't looking too good himself as he stepped from the van into the cool night air and forced a small burp and then acted as if he had tasted something awful.

Gail rushed Amber into the church and began making repairs to the costume. Wade and Jason walked toward the church. "Are you going to be all right?" Wade asked as they stopped outside the door, far enough from the building to avoid offending people should Jason have a release into the atmosphere.

"I think so." Jason covered his mouth and burped. "Ever since I ate that pepper this morning, my stomach has felt funny, and now I have these gas pains." Jason burped again and stepped away from Wade. "I'm sorry about what happened in the van, but I did try to stay home."

Wade placed his arm around Jason's shoulder. "I know you did. But you do realize that your mother has put a lot of effort into making this family reunion work."

"I know she has."

"Just remember that it will only be for a few more days, and then things should return to normal." He took his arm from around Jason's shoulder, and they entered the church.

Once inside, Jason said, "I don't think sitting in the front row is a good idea."

Wade chuckled. "What you need to do is stay by the back door and step outside when you feel the need. I'll take care of your mother and her desire that the family sit together."

Gail soon joined the family from backstage. "Where is Jason?"

"He is at the back door."

"Why?" Gail asked, ready to bring Jason in to join them.

Wade took Gail by the arm and had her take her place. "I told Jason to stay by the door in case he needed to step outside."

"That might be a good idea, but look at all the boys back there with Jason."

The lights dimmed, and the narrator began to tell the familiar story. The play was wonderful, even though the angel's halo was bent and still hanging slightly to the left. Soon the lights were back on. The audience gave the performers gracious applause and began filing out to return home. Wade and Gail waited in the van for Jason, who soon appeared with a group of his friends.

Jason left the group and approached his parents. "I'm feeling much better now and was wondering if I could spend some time with my friends this evening."

Before Gail had a chance to deliver the opening words of her "family first" speech, Amber began pleading her case for him to go with his friends, finding support from Wade.

"I think that it would be fine for Jason to be with friends as long as he isn't too late coming home," said Wade.

Obviously outnumbered, Gail relented. "Just don't be too late."

"Thank you." Jason ran off to join his friends.

"Thank you for not making him ride with us," Amber said as she rubbed her index finger under her nose. "Do you think Jason could sleep outside tonight?"

Gail found it impossible to keep from laughing, and soon the three of them were enjoying a good laugh at Jason's expense. During the drive home Gail used the mirror on the sun visor to check on Amber. Seeing Amber playing with her doll gave Gail a peaceful feeling.

Suddenly, Gail turned to Wade with a start. "I never had a chance to talk to Mother!" She paused thoughtfully. "Do you still think that I should tell her?"

Wade reached out and placed his hand on her knee. "You thought it was a good idea last night that you talk to her. Isn't that why I spent the better part of my day taking your brothers around town shopping?"

Gail sat back in her seat. "I wanted to talk to her, but things came up. Then by the time I had a chance to be alone with her, she and Dad had left for home." She was silent for a moment. "Maybe what happened today was an omen. Maybe I'm not supposed to tell her."

Wade smiled his warm, reassuring smile and winked at her. "We both know that she deserves to know. You need to talk to her about it today, before she goes to bed, or she will never forgive you."

"You're probably right." Gail stared out the windshield.

"I'm right, and you know it." Wade reached out and placed his hand on hers.

"Yes, I know you're right." Gail started to formulate several plans to find a moment alone with her mother. She hoped that only one plan would be needed, but the way things were going, she had to be prepared.

Plan A was to intercept her mother on arrival. That plan failed before it had a chance. Her parents arrived with Jerry and Lisa, who were having a conversation with her parents while helping them carry armloads of gifts from the car. The conversation continued well after the gifts found a home beneath the Christmas tree.

Plan B was to find time alone with her mother while preparing the evening meal. No one else had volunteered with any of the other meals, so why would they start now? Gail went to the refrigerator and removed the components for the meal, planning to ask her mother to join her once she was ready to start cooking. As the water for the vegetables began to boil, she was surprised to find she wasn't alone.

"Gail Rollins, what are you doing?"

Gail turned to see her mother with Jerry and Lisa. "I'm cooking tonight's meal."

"You're cooking the meal by yourself?" The tone of her mother's voice made Gail feel as if she had done something wrong.

"Once the water was boiling, I was going to ask for some help."

"Well, it's too late for that now. You run along. We are going to prepare the meal."

Gail left the kitchen under her mother's watchful eye. Lisa didn't look thrilled and was most likely there because both she and Jerry had been told they were going to help. *So much for Plan B*, thought Gail as she wondered what Plan C was going to look like.

Later in the evening, as the family was gathered by the fireplace, Gail looked for an opportunity to get her mother alone. She decided to ask her mother for help with making some refreshments.

"I'll help as well," Lisa said, placing Brandon on Jerry's lap and making her way to the kitchen.

Gail was dismayed that the only time she actually wanted Lisa to stay on the couch and do nothing was the time Lisa wanted to look helpful. She wondered what her mother might have said to make this change in Lisa. She was happy to see her willing to help, just not right now. Plan C was doomed to fail, so Gail formulated Plan D as she worked with her mother to prepare the candy-cane hot chocolate and arrange an assortment of Christmas shortbreads, Christmas tree–shaped sugar cookies, and homemade chocolates on a tray.

Lisa appeared quite content to prepare the grape concoction for Brandon and simply eavesdrop on what was being said. Gail was fairly certain that Lisa was there only to hear whether Gail would share stories of the day's incidents, so the conversation was mostly small talk, with Gail unable to bring up the subject she dearly wanted to discuss with her mother.

They returned with hot chocolate and Christmas goodies for all, and Lisa brought Brandon his grape drink. Gail's father took out his *Book of Christmas* and began to read the story of the Savior's birth and remind the family of how grateful they should be.

Everyone laughed at the dog's antics as he begged for attention and did tricks for treats. It was obvious that the best place for crumbs was near Brandon, where a constant stream of cookie pieces hit the floor, but the dog left those untouched and kept a safe distance.

The front door opened and then closed with a distinct thud, followed by the familiar sound of feet hitting every second step going upstairs. Jason never came home this early when he was with his friends, so Gail wondered what might have happened. She followed Jason up the stairs and knocked on his door.

"Is everything okay?"

She could hear sobbing but no verbal response. Opening the door a crack, she saw Jason lying on his bed with his face buried deep in his pillow. Gail entered the room and sat beside him. She slowly rubbed his back. "What happened?"

With a loud sniffle Jason raised his head. "It's your fault!" He then reburied his face in the pillow.

"How is it my fault?"

Jason's words were muffled. "If you'd made me come home with you, none of this would have happened." He lifted his head and scowled at her. "It's your fault!"

Gail rubbed his back in a slow, relaxing rhythm. "So what happened?"

"Ross embarrassed me. He said hurtful things about me in front of the girls."

She felt bad for her son but could think of nothing to say that would make him feel better. Without a word she held her breath, stopped rubbing his back, and left the room.

When Gail rejoined the family, her mother was going through the list of breakfast requests made for the following morning. Still not convinced that doing the special orders was a good idea, Gail kept her disagreement to herself and remained silent. Listening to the adults place their orders for a special breakfast too disappointed Gail and made her feel like a failure as a host. As she slipped through various emotions that eventually led to disgust over the whole ordeal, Gail came up with Plan D. She quietly slipped away and gathered up all the breakfast ingredients. Gail carried them out into the garage and hid them in a box under some old newspapers and recycling before returning to hear the discussion about how wonderful breakfast was going to be.

"I just checked the kitchen," she said as she reentered the room, "and there aren't enough supplies to make much of anything." Gail knew that she was a terrible liar but hoped to hold it together. "Maybe we should just do cold cereal in the morning."

Murmurs filled the air as the plans for the anticipated breakfast seemed to go on hold.

"Nonsense. There's enough food in this house to feed a small army," her mother muttered as she headed to the kitchen. After some banging and thumping of cupboard and pantry doors, she returned, shaking her head. "I could've sworn there was enough food to do this."

As Gail waited for her mother to stop talking about the lack of food and her disappointment at not being able to fulfill her promise to cook breakfast, she questioned whether her actions had been appropriate or just selfish. "There's still time to go shopping if we hurry," she said. "Shall we go?" Gail grabbed her keys from the shelf, and her mother moved to join her.

Lisa reached for her coat. "I need to pick up a few things as well."

Gail's grip on the keys tightened. She wanted time alone with her mother, and once again Lisa was getting in the way. Not wanting to cause a scene, Gail smiled. "The more the merrier."

But before the trio could leave, loud screams came from Amber's room. Gail rushed to her daughter's room, where she saw Amber and Brandon squared off, pushing and yelling at each other.

"What's going on?" Gail demanded as she entered the room.

Amber was almost in tears as she hugged Gail's leg. "He thinks that he's going to sleep by the fish tonight. I told him to leave so I could go to bed, and he told me no." Amber's eyes were pleading, and her voice was full of emotion. "Please make him leave."

The store was going to close soon, and there was no time to waste. Gail took Brandon by the hand. "You need to leave so Amber can go to bed. You can see the fish in the morning."

He pulled his hand from hers and ran to Lisa, who had just entered the room. "No! I want to sleep with the fish."

Lisa knelt down and took Brandon in her arms. "We need to leave so Amber can go to bed."

"No! I want to sleep with the fish!"

The more Lisa tried to reason with him, the more determined he became. With Brandon punching and kicking to get away, his tantrum grew louder. Frustration was evident for both mother and child when Lisa asked, "Can Brandon please sleep in here tonight?"

The first response came from Amber, and she was adamant. "I want him out of my room!"

Gail knew one way to change Amber's mind but was uncertain whether it would be appropriate. Brandon was not giving in, and the stores would be closing soon, so she offered Amber a bribe. "If you let Brandon sleep on the floor tonight, I will buy you more fish."

There was a long hesitation. "How many fish?"

"How many would you like?" Gail asked, hoping for a speedy resolution. She also hoped that Lisa would stay home to put Brandon to bed instead of going shopping with them.

"I want two hundred fish." Amber folded her arms. "Two hundred fish, and Brandon can sleep on my floor."

Gail saw the resolve and knew that Amber was looking to score big. "Two hundred fish is too many for your tank. How about five of those really pretty fish you like?"

"The ones that Daddy says are too expensive?"

"Those ones," Gail said without hesitation. "If you let Brandon sleep on your floor tonight, I will buy you those fish."

Amber looked pleased with the offer. "Brandon can sleep in my room, but no grape drink."

Gail sensed a victory of sorts and showed Lisa where the bedding was to make the small bed. "Mom and I will go for groceries while you're putting Brandon to bed."

Before Gail had a chance to leave, Lisa asked, "Could you make the bed while I get Brandon ready?"

Finding time to speak with her mother should have been easy. But the shopping was only an excuse to find that time alone, and she didn't want it to appear that she was trying to ditch Lisa. "I can do that, but then I have to go." Gail quickly made the little bed and, as per Amber's instructions, made sure that it was on the correct side of the line of tape.

Lisa returned with Brandon. The wires coming out of Brandon's pajamas were hard to miss, and Gail hoped that Amber wouldn't notice them. She tried to distract Amber, but it was too late.

"What is that?" Amber asked as she pointed to the control box in Lisa's hand.

Lisa tried to ignore the question and finished tucking Brandon in for the night. She soon found that ignoring Amber's question was a bad idea as Amber became insistent. Lisa kissed Brandon on the forehead and said, "This box helps keep Brandon dry during the night."

"Dry? Why? What happens? What gets wet? Will it stain my carpet?"

Before Amber could fire off any more questions than the ones that already had Lisa at a loss for words, Gail took Amber in her arms. "Brandon is a big boy who is out of diapers, but from time to time, he has an accident when he sleeps. What this little box does is wake him up before an accident happens. So there is nothing to worry about."

The look on Amber's face told Gail that she had her doubts, but it also told her that Amber was thinking about something. Gail had to wait only a few moments to learn what she was thinking.

"If something happens, will you buy me more fish?"

Tucking Amber into bed, Gail said, "If anything happens, I will buy you more fish, but nothing will happen. Trust me."

Gail and Lisa walked down the stairs, where Gail's mother was waiting with her coat and a shopping list that seemed to have grown.

"Thank you for helping convince Amber to let Brandon stay near the fish," said Lisa. She reached for her coat but then stopped. "One of us should stay to make sure nothing happens before they have fallen asleep. Could you buy a bottle of Brandon's grape drink for me?"

"I would be happy to do that for you."

Pulling into the store parking lot, Gail had many things running through her mind. Before bringing up the main issue she needed to discuss with her mother, she had to stop her mother from ranting about the missing food.

Gail put the car in park. "Enough about the missing food. I hid the food."

"You did what?"

"I hid the food in the garage to give us a reason to leave the house so we could talk." Gail was ready to tell her story when a small child throwing a serious temper tantrum outside of the store reminded her that they had to buy some grape drink mix for Lisa.

One hundred thirty dollars' worth of food, to make it look as if they actually had needed to go shopping, and a lot of small talk later, they left the store.

Gail was upset with herself as she started the van. All this time together, and she still hadn't told her mother about the meeting, and even now, she still wondered when the right time would be. She put the van in gear and did a shoulder check. And then she put the van back in park. "Mom, I have something I need to tell you."

"Are you pregnant?"

The look on Gail's face must have been priceless because her normally reserved mother started to laugh uncontrollably.

"No!" Gail said. "But it is about a child."

"What child?" her mother asked.

"Me."

"What? You are no child."

"I was when you adopted me."

Gail's mother was curious. "And what do you need to tell me?"

Gail could scarcely contain her excitement. "I think I found my birth mother." Gail watched her mother's expression and was pleased to see her smile.

"When? How? Where? Have you met her?" the questions came fast enough to rival Amber.

When the initial questions had been asked, and several hugs shared, Gail said, "They contacted me last night with a phone call.

Gail's mother had a puzzled expression. "I thought Dale was the one who called last night?"

Gail smiled. "We have call waiting. The call came just as I was saying good-bye to Dale."

"So when are you going to meet her?"

Gail could hear the excitement in her mother's voice. "We are going to meet Tuesday night at the food court in the mall."

"Wonderful dear, I have always wondered what she is like, and now we will finally get to know."

They lost track of time as they shared the moment. Gail was happy that she had taken the time to talk with her mother even though it would have been so easy to let the opportunity slip away.

When they returned home, the only family waiting up for them was Wade. He joked that Gail's father had been ready to call the police and send out a search party until he found out what was going on. And then he'd just gone to bed.

Gail's mother looked at the clock. "I don't blame him. Look at the time, morning is going to come soon enough, especially breakfast." She handed Wade the bag of groceries she was holding and went to her room.

"You told Dad?" Gail gave Wade a hug and handed him a bag of groceries. "How did he take the news?"

"He is quite excited at the prospect of being part of the meeting tomorrow night." Wade looked inside the grocery bag. "Did you have to buy so much food on a pretend shopping trip?"

Gail didn't acknowledge his remark about the food. "The meeting tomorrow is only for the two of us." Her eyes grew wide as she placed her hand over her mouth. "I wonder if Mom thinks she is coming as well, even though I never invited her to come."

Wade rearranged the refrigerator to make room for the items that needed to be kept cold. He ate some Christmas baking and justified the tall glass of milk to empty the carton as necessary to make room for the extra food. Wade placed the rest of the groceries on the kitchen counter before he turned off the light. "We can talk to your parents in the morning. Right now it's time for bed." He gave a big yawn and stretched his hands high above his head. "These late nights are killing me."

Chapter Seven

GAIL'S SLEEP THAT NIGHT, if it could be considered sleep, was restless and unsettled. She tossed and turned with worry about how her parents might react when told that the planned meeting was a closed affair. Exhaustion finally brought sleep to Gail's troubled mind, but it came much too late and was much too short. Gail's brief rest was disturbed when the tranquility of the morning was shattered at 5:34 a.m. by bloodcurdling screams from Amber's room.

Wade and Gail jumped out of bed and rushed to Amber's room. They opened the door and heard a strange buzzing sound that was audible only between Amber's still frantic screams. In the glow of the hallway night-light, they could see Amber struggling to free herself from the sheets.

Sprawled across the middle of the bed was Brandon. The buzzing noise was the bed-wetting alarm, which hadn't woken him from his sleep. A closer look at Amber showed her pajamas to be completely soaked. Amber was shaking, at least in part from being wet, but Gail was sure it was more from the disgusting thought of being in a urine-soaked bed. Gail went to Amber's aid and freed her from the sheets. She took her daughter in her arms and held her close. The urge for Gail to pull away from the soggy clothes was instinctive, but she continued to comfort her daughter by holding her close and speaking softly in her ear.

Lisa rushed in and turned off the alarm. "It must have been the sound of running water that caused this to happen. Brandon has been good for weeks."

Gail could only shake her head as Lisa fired off one excuse after another in an attempt to spin the attention away from her son. The moment was stressful to a sleep-deprived Gail, and it only got worse.

"I told you that I didn't want him in my room last night. I told you!" Amber pulled away from Gail's chest and looked her mother squarely in the eyes. "I told you I didn't want him here in my room last night! It will take a lot more than fish to make me happy now!"

Gail placed her hand over Amber's mouth and tried to quiet the child, hoping that Wade hadn't picked up on the statement.

"What about the fish?" Wade asked.

Amber blurted out, "Mommy promised to buy me fish for my tank if I would be quiet and not upset Aunt Lisa when Brandon was being bad."

Gail saw the expression on Lisa's face and the clenched jaw muscles as she stared at Amber after the comment about Brandon being bad.

"So how many fish is your mother going to buy you?" Wade asked.

Amber pretended to count on her fingers. "Mommy promised to buy me more than ten—five of them the really pretty fish that you say cost too much." Amber snuggled back into her mother's arms. She was silent a few seconds. "Mommy, you don't have to worry about buying more fish for the wet bed."

"I don't?"

"No, for this I want a sister!"

Gail could feel a blush coming. "You want a sister?"

"Yes, but not a baby sister that will cry all night and wet the bed. I want a big sister like Vicki. She's nice!"

Gail quickly changed the subject. "It's time to give Amber a bath."

Gail finished bathing Amber, started a load of laundry, and then had her own shower before heading downstairs for breakfast. She had been totally prepared to enjoy cold cereal, but the aromas that wafted through the house were heavenly and reminded Gail of breakfasts growing up. When she arrived in the kitchen, her mother was cooking up a storm. There were scrambled eggs, pancakes, omelets, waffles, hash-brown potatoes, bacon—lots of bacon—and many other items from the family's list of requests. The flurry of activity was one that would make any short-order cook proud. Dishes of food were placed in front of the children, and Jason started to eat as if he hadn't eaten in weeks. Amber and Brandon, on the other hand, both looked at the food on their plates, picked at it, and then asked for a bowl of cold cereal.

Unable to shake her headache or the mood she was in, Gail said, "I told you so!" and went to the garage.

Wade waited a few minutes before joining his wife, to give her some time alone with her thoughts. When he finally entered the garage, Gail had the workout gloves on and was delivering a severe beating to the punching bag.

"I do hope that I'm not the reason for the sudden urge to exercise," joked Wade as he stepped behind the bag to brace it.

Gail lashed out with a flurry of punches, with an intensity he had never seen before.

"So how has the reunion been for you up until now?"

Gail didn't say a word as she landed a punch close to his nose.

Wade stepped back from the bag. "It's been that good?"

Gail took a break from releasing her frustrations to speak with Wade. The longer they talked, the more relaxed she became, and she began to see the humor of the events, humor that had escaped her while she was trying to make things right.

Wade put his arms around Gail and gave her a kiss. "Your siblings and parents are adults, and you need to realize that they can—and should—fend for themselves. You don't need to babysit them!"

Amber entered the garage. "Mommy, Daddy, come quick!"

"What is it, sweetheart? Did Brandon do something?" She felt guilty about blaming Brandon without knowing what had happened.

"Yes."

"Then his mother should take care of it."

"You need to come because she is busy."

Gail stepped away from Wade's embrace and pushed the punching bag. "What is she doing?" she asked Amber.

"Aunt Lisa started a fight with Uncle Dale."

After assuring Amber that she would be right behind her, Gail took another punch at the bag and gave a grunt of disgust. She turned to Wade. "So! My family is adult enough to take care of themselves, are they?"

"I thought they were," Wade said as he shrugged his shoulders.

"Well, obviously, you thought wrong."

Wade smiled. "So what are you going to do?"

"I'm not sure what I am going to do." Gail unleashed another flurry of punches. "If it weren't for this punching bag to beat on, I am afraid that I would punch the annoying bag that truly deserves it—and my brothers!" Gail was exasperated as she gave the bag a parting kick and began to remove the gloves. When she turned and saw Amber still standing in the garage, she swallowed hard. She wondered how much she had understood of the last statements or how much she didn't understand and would question later. There was little time to wonder because now Jason appeared in the garage, telling them to hurry.

Gail rushed to the kitchen with visions of knife-wielding relatives threatening each other across the table while the rest of the family cowered in fear. What she found was a very unconcerned Brandon sitting at the table with several partially filled bowls of cereal, much like the previous morning. Lisa was yelling at Dale about minding his own business where the upbringing of her son was concerned, and Dale, on the other hand, was showing no signs of trying to resolve the situation in any diplomatic fashion.

Jerry was trying to separate the two of them before they came to blows by holding Lisa from behind, with her arms trapped by his. One part of what Gail had envisioned was accurate: the rest of the family cowering in fear. Her parents were in the hallway, watching with concern but in no obvious hurry to intervene.

With a sharp, piercing voice usually reserved for her own children when the situation called for it, Gail entered the kitchen and exclaimed, "What is going on here?"

Silence filled the room as it did with her own children when Gail was upset. Gail demanded answers, and everyone remained silent.

Finally, Amber spoke up. "Uncle Dale told Aunt Lisa to stop spoiling Brandon by giving in to him all the time. He told her to make him eat what was placed in front of him instead of wasting all the food."

Gail looked at Dale. "Is that true?"

"Yes, I said that."

Gail looked at Lisa. "So what's the problem here?"

Lisa remained silent, ignoring Gail as best she could while glaring at Dale.

"Jason, you take Amber and Brandon to play in the other room, and watch them so nothing else happens while we are busy." Gail waited until the children were gone before she addressed her family. "The rest of you, sit down around the table!"

In Gail's opinion family negotiations required the same amount of diplomacy as would be required during negotiations between warring superpowers. Gail's biggest problem in these peace talks was that the experienced diplomat was one of the warring parties.

Gail had to start somewhere and figured Lisa was a good choice to go first.

"Lisa, would you please tell the family what has you upset."

Lisa sat silent without any indication she was going to respond. After several minutes of silence with everyone looking at her, she decided to speak. "I am so tired of Brandon being wrongfully blamed when something goes wrong. He is only three years old after all."

Gail looked at her brother. "Dale, would you please share your concerns with us."

Dale cleared his throat. "I have observed a trend. It seems that Lisa only knows what is going on with her son, after something has happened. Then, without looking into the situation, she simply starts making excuses for her son while blaming others. My concern is that she needs to be a more responsible mother for Brandon while she is here." Dale was cut off.

"Lisa is a very good mother and is taking good care of our son." Jerry said, as he stood to approach Dale.

Dale continued, "Lisa can catch all of her shows, at home, after the reunion, when they are on re-run."

Gail took a deep breath and wished that she had left her siblings to work out their differences – alone. The ensuing discussion was heated, and at times close to having punches thrown. Lisa and Jerry must have felt like they were being ganged up on, and fought back to defend not only Brandon's actions, but Lisa's as well.

Finally, the conversation became more civil, and they started to sound like a close, loving family. They even thanked Gail for what she was doing. No sooner had the family started to laugh at their pettiness than Amber entered the kitchen with one of her thoughtful expressions that always preceded a series of questions.

Having averted a family war and possibly salvaged the rest of the reunion, Gail moved quickly toward Amber. She hoped to whisk Amber safely from the kitchen before any words left her mouth. She came close but did not quite make it.

"I looked all over the house and could only find the punching bag in the garage. I never did find the annoying bag that you want to beat on."

The silence in the kitchen was deafening. "There is only one bag to beat on, and it is the punching bag in the garage," Gail said as she left the kitchen with Amber in tow.

Later, the remains of what should have been a happy breakfast were barely put away when Jason announced that he was hungry. Gail pulled some dishes of Mexican food from the fridge and placed them in front of him. "Enjoy!"

Jason looked woefully at the dishes. "If I eat another bite of this food, I will start speaking like a native Mexican and will probably start to swear." Jason reached for the closest dish, took a bite, and started to mutter in the broken Spanish he remembered from school.

Not knowing whether Amber's comment about the punching bag had been taken badly was stressful for Gail. She entered the room where Jerry and Lisa were watching TV to start what she hoped would be a friendly conversation during a commercial. The conversation felt friendly, but as she had discovered earlier, her family members were good at hiding their emotions and letting them fester. The show resumed, and Gail was ready to leave when Dale entered the room carrying Amber. She looked ready to cry and was rubbing her eyes.

"What's wrong, sweetheart?" Gail asked as she took Amber from Dale.

"I have a headache."

Gail felt her daughter's forehead and was satisfied that it wasn't a fever. "Do you have a tired headache?"

Any doubts about the status quo in the house were erased in a heartbeat as Lisa ignored her television program to join the conversation. "You're not going to blame this headache on my son being in her room last night. He went right to sleep and, as we found out, slept very soundly."

Gail felt a headache of her own starting to form as she searched for a polite way to prevent yet another heated family discussion. Gail was carefully planning her response to Lisa when she was interrupted by Amber.

"Brandon didn't keep me awake."

Lisa jumped at the chance. "I am so tired of everyone jumping to conclusions and blaming Brandon for the bad things that happen." She was continuing on her tirade, making her opinions and frustrations with the situation known, when she too was interrupted by Amber.

"Brandon didn't keep me awake. It was Aunt Lisa!" By this time Amber was crying and holding her head.

Lisa went silent. The entire family was now in the room, having heard the sounds of the latest outpouring of love and family unity. With her voice now very subdued, Lisa asked, "How did I keep you awake last night? I was in my room."

Amber rubbed her eyes. "You and Uncle Jerry were laughing and playing all night."

Jerry had a concerned look on his face as he stood up. "Gail, you really need to put your daughter down for a nap. Look how red her eyes are becoming." He reached for Lisa's hand to help her from the couch. "We need to go buy some fish for Amber's fish tank to replace the ones that died in the grape drink."

"You need to go buy them right now?" Wade asked as a smile formed on his face. "We don't even know what kinds Amber wants."

"We need to go while there is still a good selection," Jerry said as he tried to slip past Wade.

"I'm sure there will be plenty of fish in the store if you go later." Wade motioned for Jerry to take a seat. "I think it's safe to say that we are all in agreement that Brandon was not responsible for keeping Amber awake last night." He looked around the room. "However, I do believe that if Brandon were to sleep in the same room as his parents, everyone would get a better night's sleep."

Chapter Eight

FOR THE REST OF the day, Jerry and Lisa were model parents as they took care of Brandon. Amber had been adamant that Brandon was not to be in her room with the fish while she had a nap. Brandon had been vocal in his displeasure at not being able to see the fish and had thrown a tantrum. Gail wasn't sure if she had actually heard what she thought she heard in their room, but she could have sworn that the tantrum earned Brandon a spanking. She smiled. Relative peace had returned to the Rollins home, and the family appeared to be enjoying their time together.

Dale had the keys to Wade's car as he passed Gail in the hallway. "Sorry to duck out, but I just received a call and have to leave on more official business."

Gail was disappointed that Dale was going to leave the family again and tried to make eye contact with him. "Are you going to the embassy again?"

"Yes I am."

Gail sighed. "Is that girl always this needy?"

Dale avoided making eye contact as he reached for his coat. "Consuela is a friend going through a rough time and needs someone to talk to."

"Where is her mother?"

"Her mother is there but not very supportive of the decision to cancel the wedding. She really likes Ramón, and had she been one of the bridesmaids, I'm fairly certain that

Consuela would have had reason to send her packing as well."

The unexpected visual made Gail shiver. "I can see how awkward that could be, but we really would like you here with us."

"I really do want to spend time with the family, but Consuela is like family." Dale pulled the collar of his coat around his face and reached for the door handle. "Living in the desert really makes this weather feel colder than it should." He turned to Gail. "I promise that I will return to join the family for the evening meal."

The afternoon slipped into evening. Gail was excited about the upcoming meeting but was becoming more nervous. She expressed her apprehension to Wade during a quiet conversation. Gail had spent a great deal of time trying on several different outfits and then deeming each outfit inappropriate for one reason or another. Gail finally settled on the first pair of navy blue pants and white sweater that she had tried on.

Her mother met Gail and Wade at the door as they were preparing to leave. "I do wish that I could join you."

"I wish you could join us too, but they wanted it to be a small gathering, not a media event."

Tears were visible in her mother's eyes, and the disappointment was obvious in her voice. "I can appreciate and respect their wishes that it be a small gathering. But I really would like to meet her." She gave Gail a big hug. "Pictures would be nice. Maybe the two of you could pose on Santa's knee."

They shared a small laugh about having a picture with Santa. Gail could only imagine how much being part of the meeting would have meant to her mother and wished that she could be part of it. The last thing Gail saw as they drove away was her mother waving from the window.

* * * * *

Jerry looked up to see his mother enter the den as he watched the hockey game with his father. For as long as he could remember, she had never bothered to try talking with his father during the games because he ignored the world while he watched, especially when his two favorite teams were involved, like today's game.

"I have some last-minute shopping to do, and we need to go to the mall."

Jerry's father never looked away from the screen. "Have fun."

The whistle blew to stop the action, and his mother took the opportunity. "We need to go to the mall right this instant!"

The puck dropped, and play resumed. Exasperated by her husband's lack of cooperation, Jerry's mother stood in front of the screen so that it was impossible to see the game. "I need you to take me to the mall this instant!"

Jerry watched the interaction of his parents. With his mother in front of the screen, his father leaned to the left to see around her. When she moved to block his view, he simply leaned the other direction. Then when it appeared that he had tired of the inconvenience, he stood and moved her to the side.

With the next stoppage of play, his father looked up. "What could we possibly need to purchase? There are enough gifts under the tree to open a small store."

When she moved back in front of the screen and planted her hands on her hips, Jerry knew that his mother meant business. The way his father folded his arms and looked at the screen instead of his wife told Jerry he might want to leave them alone for this conversation.

"We need to go to the mall right now!"

"What possible reason could you have to go to the mall? The crowds of last-minute shoppers will make it a zoo in there. Besides, you told Gail that you would take care of the kids while they were out." His team scored a goal, and he shifted from side to side to catch a glimpse of the replay.

She turned off the game. "You would rather watch a stupid game than take me to the mall?"

There was a moment of silence. "You mean …?" He never finished his question but apparently knew he had his answer by his wife's response. He stood up and went for his coat and keys.

Jerry knew that his father would rather cut off a limb than miss watching his favorite team play. When the game was abandoned so easily, he became curious and followed them. "So what's up?"

"We have to go shopping," his mother said again.

The sharp look from his mother prompted Jerry to push for information that wasn't readily forthcoming. "What's really going on?"

"We need to go shopping, and you and Lisa need to take care of the kids."

"Not until you tell me. Dad would never leave a hockey game without a good reason. So what is going on?"

"If we don't leave now, we will miss everything."

"So tell me, and you can go."

Her husband was waiting at the open front door, and precious time was being wasted, so Jerry's mother told him what was happening. "Gail is meeting her birth mother at the mall food court in a few minutes. If we hurry, we might find a good vantage point in the store window across from the food court."

"Won't Gail be disappointed if you crash her party?" Jerry asked.

"Not as disappointed as I will be if I miss seeing the meeting. Now get out of my way."

Jerry stepped aside to let her past.

Before they left, his mother said seriously, "I told you this in confidence. Not a word to anyone."

Just then, Lisa arrived to see why there was such a draft of cold air coming down the hallway. She was intrigued by what she had heard. "What are we being sworn to secrecy about?"

Jerry's mother scowled at Lisa and pointed at Jerry. "Not a word!"

The interrogation that ensued from Lisa after the door closed was intense and unrelenting. Feeling that sharing what he knew would be of little consequence, Jerry told Lisa what his mother had told him. No sooner had the words left his mouth than Lisa reached for her coat and handed Jerry his. Jerry tried to stop the escape. "We have been left in charge and are supposed to feed the kids."

Jerry could tell that Lisa had made up her mind. She was going to be a spectator to Gail's reunion, and nothing was going to stop her. In response to his reminder that they needed to feed the children, she simply said, "Let them eat Mexican."

Jerry went to Jason's room and knocked. He knew better than to just walk in, so he waited for permission to enter. Once that all important permission was granted he opened the door. "Jason, something has come up and I need you to feed Amber and Brandon while we are out."

Jason looked up from his computer game. "Why me, where is everyone else?"

"Dale is still at the embassy and the rest of the adults need to be somewhere right now."

Jason paused his game, and leaned back in his chair. "Mom told me that I couldn't make any plans with my friends this week because the family is to spend time together." He leaned back further and clasped his hands behind his head. "Now everyone is gone and I'm stuck here with the kids."

Lisa called from the front door. "Jerry, we need to go!"

Jerry looked at Jason. "This is adult together time so I really need you to take charge."

Lisa called again and was emphatic when she said that they had to hurry.

Jason pushed way from his desk. "Fine I'll do it this time. What am I supposed to feed them?"

"I don't know. There are a lot of leftovers…"

"We are not going to eat Mexican!" Jason said, as he sat down on his chair.

Lisa called a third time. "Jerry, we need to go - now!"

"Lisa and I have to go. Amber and Brandon are in looking at the fish, and I don't care what you feed them, just feed them."

As Jerry and Lisa headed toward the front door, it opened. As promised, Dale had returned from his official business to spend time with family at the evening meal. Jerry was relieved to see him. "You are in charge and need to make sure the kids are fed."

"Where is everyone? Gail made me promise to be home in time to spend the evening with the family."

"They all had to leave, and so do we," Lisa said as she buttoned her coat. "Jerry needs to take me to the mall."

"What's the big rush?" Dale asked as Lisa pulled Jerry toward the door.

To save his sanity, Jerry told Dale what was happening and managed to finish the story before Lisa closed the door, exclaiming, "We are going to be late!"

Dale smacked his fist against the door frame in frustration as he realized that the entire rest of his family would be a part of a special moment for Gail, even though their participation would be like a bunch of Peeping Toms spying on her. He wanted to go but knew that the children and their endless need for food needed to be taken care of. In the kitchen he found Jason serving up a can of smoked oysters.

"Why are you feeding them something they won't like when there is so much other food in the house?" Dale asked as he watched Brandon spit the chewy ball of protein onto the floor.

"Because they won't eat any more Mexican food, and I refuse to eat another bite of it myself!" Jason placed an oyster in his mouth, chewed it, and made no attempt to hide his lack of enjoyment.

Dale could sympathize with Jason about the excessive consumption of ethnic leftovers. He also saw a window of opportunity. "Jason, have I got a deal for you!"

"What kind of deal?" Jason asked as he tossed the can of oysters in the trash.

Dale placed his credit card on the counter. "I'm going to leave my credit card so that you can order in some food for the children while I am gone."

"Where are Mom and everyone else?"

"They went out and left me in charge of making sure the three of you are fed." He looked at Jason and slid the card closer. "I'm asking you to help me feed the children by ordering something they will eat. Order some pizza or whatever. Can you do this for me?"

"Does everyone want pizza?" Jason asked. The other children cheered their approval. He turned to Dale. "I'll do it."

Dale couldn't believe how busy the mall traffic still was at this hour. He circled the parking lot several times before he finally found a parking space, one he almost lost to an aggressive young mother in a beat-up subcompact car. Once inside the mall, he found a map. Hoping that he wasn't too late and that he could find a good vantage point from which to observe the meeting, he approached the food court. He was in luck. Gail and Wade were just walking toward a table with another couple.

In the first store window with a view, he saw his mother nestled into the seasonal display like a live mannequin waving to shoppers passing by. When he stopped and pointed at her, she began to wave at him—not a friendly wave but one with purpose as she tried to get him to move on. In the next window display, he saw his father in a perfect vantage point, without his glasses, straining to see what was happening. Dale was disappointed when the next suitable window was covered with paper. The next store window had Lisa and Jerry on display. They were posing as parents watching children opening gifts, and there was no room for a third observer. Dale came to the final store window that gave him any chance for a clean line of sight.

He looked at the window display and swallowed hard. He questioned whether his desire to watch his sister was worth entering the store. All his life, he had been taught to avoid the appearance of evil, and the teaching had served him well both personally and professionally. But Dale was a desperate man because he wanted to get out of sight and still be able to watch Gail's meeting. He rationalized his actions by telling himself that it would be all right since he had no intentions of doing any shopping; besides, nobody would recognize him. Dale quickly debated the dilemma before him and made his choice. Dale reached his hands deep into his overcoat pockets, looked both ways as if he was about to cross a busy street, and walked into the store selling ladies' intimate clothing.

"May I be of service to you?" asked the girl behind the counter as she watched Dale very closely with her finger poised over the silent alarm button.

Dale flashed his credentials. "I'm on official government business." He allowed the salesgirl to examine the credentials. "I need to use your display window for a stakeout."

"You need to do what?"

Dale turned toward the window full of scantily clad mannequins. "I need to use your display window for a stakeout."

The girl smiled at him and winked. "Help yourself and take all the time you need. I will be right here if you have any questions."

His first attempt to find a vantage point resulted in his disrobing a mannequin by simply brushing the outfit with his arm. He picked up the garment from the floor and wondered what a real piece of clothing would cost when he saw the price tag. His thoughts were interrupted by another one of the salesgirls, who adjusted the Santa hat as she redressed the mannequin.

"There is no need to undress the display," she said. "We have plenty of the display items in stock."

Dale questioned the wisdom of coming into the store and was convinced that he had made a mistake when the salesgirl proceeded to offer her assistance.

"Sometimes the display doesn't do the clothing justice. I would be more than happy to model the clothing for you to see if it meets with your approval."

Dale gulped a couple of times and was grateful for the subdued lighting as he cleared his throat and tried to sound official. "I'm here on government business." He produced his credentials for the girl to see.

She examined the credentials and smiled. "If you do happen to find something you like while here on official government business, my offer to model it for you still stands." She returned the credentials to Dale and gave the Santa hat a final adjustment.

"Thank you for such a generous offer, but I am on a stakeout and need to get back to work." He turned to the display and tried to find a spot from which he could watch without giving the salesgirl any reason to return.

Dale found a space to look from but wasn't satisfied with the view, so he shifted a little more to the right. As he shifted even further to the right to see the entire group, he heard something hit the floor. He didn't want to know what had fallen but instinctively looked down. Dale stepped back from the window and picked the items from the floor.

He blushed as he looked at the outfit and remembered the offer of live modeling. His personal blush quickly turned to a look of horror when he turned to check on Gail and instead saw Vicki, Jason's girlfriend, and one of her girlfriends looking in at him. An uncomfortable feeling arose in the pit of his stomach when Vicki entered the store.

Vicki rubbed the fabric to her face and exclaimed, "Dale, you are a sweetheart! This is my favorite color."

The knot in his stomach tightened, and he found it difficult to breathe. Coming into the store had been a mistake, and Dale was suffering the consequence of his actions. He tried to speak but could only mouth the words "Please stop." He felt his knees weaken.

Vicki showed no mercy. "I know you said that I would be surprised by your gift, but this is beyond even my wildest expectations."

Dale wished that he could become invisible and blend into the woodwork. Vicki was a worthy adversary, and she had won this round. He had no time to feel sorry for himself and just wanted to leave. But escape was not an option because now his predicament was compounded by the return of the salesgirl.

"Would you like me to model the clothes?" she asked.

"That would be wonderful," said Vicki. "In fact, could you model these as well?" Vicki pointed to the mannequins with even more revealing outfits.

Dale knew what Vicki was doing and wasn't going to give her the satisfaction if he could help it. To prevent the situation from getting worse, he took action. "Modeling won't be necessary. I'll take this one."

The clothes were folded and placed in a gift box. Dale watched and wondered why they weren't just put into an envelope. He hoped that Vicki would leave before he had to make the purchase, but her smile told him that she was quite content watching him squirm.

"Will that be cash or charge?"

"That will be charge." Dale reached into his wallet for his credit card. He felt for the card a couple of times and then remembered leaving it with Jason. Opening a second flap where he kept his emergency stash, Dale felt the two crisp hundred-dollar bills. "I guess that it will have to be cash."

"Thank you for your business, and I do hope you remember us for your next stakeout." The salesgirl placed the package into a bag and handed it to Dale.

Dale looked at the bag and sighed. "Do you have a bag without the store logo?

The salesgirl smiled. "All of our bags and boxes have the logo. The only choice you have is the color, hot pink or cherry red."

"I'll take the cherry red bag." He stuffed the garments into the bag and proceeded to roll it as small as possible before he stuffed it into the inside pocket of his overcoat.

The incident with Vicki had cost Dale time and money, but he was determined that it wasn't going to cost him a chance to see Gail's mother. He entered the food court, marched up to the first counter, and ordered the Christmas special.

The girl placed a tray on the counter. Would you like the polar bear or the penguin ornament?"

Dale looked at the two choices and said, "The bear."

She placed the free ornament on his tray and said, "That will be nine dollars and sixty-five cents. How are you going to pay?""

"Cash," Dale reached into his pocket and pulled out his change. He counted the money and shook his head in disbelief. He didn't have enough money.

"Sir, your total is nine dollars and sixty-five cents."

Dale could only shake his head. "I don't have enough money."

The girl rolled her eyes. "How much money do you have?"

He held out his hand. "I have eight dollars and seventy-five cents."

She removed the free ornament from the tray. "You seem quite interested in those people in the corner."

"What people?"

"The people you keep looking at." Before Dale could even think to deny his interest in the group, she said, "I'll cover the difference for your meal and even put the ornament back on the tray if you will tell me what's going on."

"What makes you think that something is going on?"

The girl sighed. "There has to be a reason why all those people are pretending to be decorations in the store windows."

Dale turned to see things from the girl's vantage point. He saw his family on display and couldn't miss how they glared at him.

She produced the promised change. "So what is going on?"

Dale turned back to the girl. "What do you think is going on?"

"I could guess, but unless you tell me, I won't know for sure." She tapped the coins on the counter.

Dale didn't hesitate to offer an explanation. "The lady with her back to us is my sister. She is meeting with her birth mother for the first time since being given up for adoption."

"So who are those people in the store windows?"

Dale turned. "The one on the left is my mother. The squinting man in the next window is my father."

"Doesn't the poor man have glasses?"

Dale chuckled. "If you look real close you can see them on top of his head. He does that a lot."

The girl laughed. "So who is the happy couple in the other window?"

Dale smiled. "That happy couple is my brother and his wife. Only she really doesn't look too happy right now."

The girl wiped at a tear. "I can only wonder how my family will react when I find my birth mother." She placed the money into the register, slid the food tray toward Dale, and then turned away, wiping her tears with a napkin.

"I hope that you find your birth mother," Dale said as he watched her disappear from view.

Dale turned toward Gail and her birth mother. There was a definite resemblance, but most telling were the similar nervous mannerisms they shared. One last look at the store windows told Dale that some might feel that he had overstayed his welcome, so he left.

The drive home allowed him to find the humor in the clothing store experience with Vicki. He was still upset about having to make a purchase but had to smile at how skillfully Vicki had controlled the situation. She and the salesgirl had left him no other recourse but to make the purchase. It hurt to think how much he had paid for so little, but it was only money.

What he wouldn't get over so quickly was the encounter with the girl at the food court. He'd never had to experience the yearning to know what his birth parents were like because he had known them all his life. He'd never had to wonder what it would mean to belong to a loving birth family because he had one. Dale began to realize that he had taken too many things in life for granted.

Dale pulled up in front of the house and saw a delivery van drive away, only to be replaced by a pizza delivery car. Dale looked at his watch and noted that it had taken a long time for the food to be delivered. He watched as Jason received the food and paid with the credit card like an old pro. He wondered what mood the kids were going to be in and decided to remain outside long enough for the kids to devour the food.

Jerry and Lisa were the next to return, and Jerry approached Dale outside. "What were you thinking? You let Gail see you. Gail is going to be so upset because of you."

It felt like old times, where Jerry tried to blame everything on Dale. "Why would she be upset at me? All I did was order some food and talk with the girl serving me."

"What did you talk about? I saw you looking at us."

"She wanted to know if I knew why people were in the store windows." Dale smiled. "You weren't very well hidden."

Jerry pushed Dale's shoulder. "We were well hidden as part of the display. You didn't even try to hide and deliberately showed yourself."

Dale did not react to the push. Instead, he stood still and reminded himself just how lucky he was to have such a loving family.

"I told you of the meeting in the strictest of confidence. Even you, a junior diplomat, should know what that means!" Jerry said, his voice beginning to rise.

Lisa came up beside her husband and placed her arm around his. "Keep it down. The neighbors are watching."

Dale knew that his brother had more to say by the bulging blood vessel but wasn't going to say it in the presence of his wife.

"You never said it was in the strictest of confidence," Dale said. "When you wanted to leave so badly, Lisa offered the information voluntarily and not in the strictest of confidence." Dale laughed as he motioned toward the approaching car. "If you were told about the meeting in strictest confidence, you should be concerned about what to tell Mom. As for me, I went shopping without any prior knowledge of the meeting, and I have a package to prove it."

It was evident to Dale upon entering the house that there could be a discussion about some of the evening's other events too. Even though the children were well behaved and sitting up to the table, sharing a cheese pizza, it was the two unopened pizza boxes from a different pizza place and the other boxes of fast food that were going to catch Gail's attention. The sight definitely caught Dale's attention when he realized that all the food had been purchased on his credit card. "Jason! How much did you spend?"

Jason looked up from his meal. "I have no idea. But the receipts are all right here." He patted a neat pile of yellow and white papers with his signature on them.

Dale reached for the receipts. His lips moved slightly as he made the calculations in his head and uttered unintelligible words from time to time. His face was flushed when he finally looked away from the papers. "Is this everything?"

The smile on Jason's face was similar to the one on Vicki's when the clothing purchase was made. "We are still waiting for the Chinese food."

"You ordered Chinese food as well?"

"Yes, we ordered a takeout meal for six because it had pineapple chicken."

Dale moved toward Jason and held the papers in his face. "The food at your mother's wedding didn't cost as much as what you have spent so far to feed three children. And you say there's still more food on the way?"

The doorbell rang, and Jason moved over to Amber to use her as a shield. "That must be the food. Would you like to sign for it, or shall I?"

Dale glared at his nephew, set the receipts on the table, and went to the door. The urge to vent his frustrations at the delivery person vanished when he found himself staring at the man's chest and then looking up to his eyes. Without saying a word, he took the clipboard and signed his name. He returned to the kitchen. "I'll bet you think that buying all this food is funny, don't you?" Dale exclaimed as he gathered the other receipts again. "With this slip the total is well over six hundred dollars."

Jason's demeanor changed as he held his ground. "This is only money, and you already know the price," Jason said. "You have absolutely no idea what it's like to be totally and completely embarrassed in front of a girl like Vicki. You can't put a price on that kind of embarrassment!"

Without batting an eye, Dale muttered, "One hundred ninety-six dollars and forty-two cents plus tax."

Jason looked hurt. "How can you joke about this? There is no way to put a price tag on hurt emotions!" Jason stormed to his room.

Dale looked at his watch and then at his parents, who had entered the house during the confrontation and were watching from the other doorway with Jerry and Lisa. "Please, enjoy the food. I need to call Amanda."

As he left the kitchen, Dale heard Amber say, "Jason even ordered more Mexican food."

* * * * *

Gail and Wade stopped at the pet store and purchased the fish Gail had promised Amber, plus a couple extra for good measure, before they returned home. Amber greeted them at the door and squealed with delight when she saw the fish. She hugged both her parents and then raced to her room.

Gail turned to Wade. "What does that smell like to you?"

Wade breathed deeply. "I think it might be Chinese pizza."

Gail sniffed the air. "It definitely doesn't smell like the meal I told mom to cook, I wonder what the children ate?"

Her suspicions were confirmed when she entered the kitchen and stepped on a fortune cookie. She stooped down to pick it up and placed it in the garbage, where she encountered many other empty food boxes. She found a container of rice on the counter and tried to place it in the fridge, but couldn't find room next to the pizza and Chinese food. She looked at Wade. "You were right. It does smell like Chinese pizza."

Gail and Wade dished up an eclectic assortment of food for supper. Wade ate a prawn. "Do you think the family is tired of Mexican food?"

"I'm not sure," Gail said as she popped a deep-fried chicken ball into her mouth.

"Neither am I." Wade grinned. "Do you think it might be a safe bet that the family wouldn't bother us to take them with us if we took a trip to Cancun right now?"

Gail acknowledged his comment but was distracted by the amount of food in the house that had not been there when they left. "You don't think that Jason was left in charge tonight, do you?"

"He might have been if Dale didn't make it home in time from seeing Consuela. But who would have bought the food?" Wade nudged Gail. "I just hope it wasn't me."

Gail knew what Wade meant but just smiled. "Maybe Dale bought the food to keep the kids quiet. I just can't imagine him buying this much."

Wade grabbed another prawn. "It's possible. Two experienced parents filled a lot of cereal bowls at breakfast."

They finished their meals and joined the family in the family room.

"So how was your shopping trip?" Lisa asked.

Gail squeezed Wade's hand. "It was good. You know, I never realized just how lifelike some window displays look."

"Really? What stores?"

"There were several interesting displays. Some were so good that they reminded me of family." Gail paused. "Enough about shopping. How was your evening without us?"

Gail knew that her parents, along with Jerry and Lisa, had been at the mall. The meeting had been a wonderful experience, and she wished that Dale could have been a part of it as well. *Maybe next time*, she thought as Dale joined them. "How is Consuela doing?"

"She is doing fine."

"Good, I'm glad to hear that." Gail wanted to press Dale for more information but thought better of it "So, everyone, how was your evening while Wade and I were out?"

The silence was deafening. However, during the silence they were able to hear the faint sounds of Christmas carols being sung. Gail loved listening to Christmas carols and went to the window. She brushed the curtains aside and saw a large group of young people sharing the spirit of the season through song. She listened and watched as this musical group worked its way along the street toward them.

When the group stopped at their house, Gail called for the family to join her. "Quick, come listen to the carolers."

When the last notes of their final carol faded into the crisp night air, the carolers wished Gail and her family a Merry Christmas.

Chapter Nine

GAIL WAS TIRED AND looking forward to a good night's rest. Today had been a good day. Meeting her birth mother for the first time had been a special treat and had answered many questions that had bothered her. She now knew why she had been given up for adoption. Wade interrupted her thoughts when he hit her with a pillow.

"Are you coming to bed, or is there something we need to discuss all night?"

Gail smiled and grabbed her pillow. The fight was on.

Wade surrendered after a couple of blows and took Gail in his arms. "I love you, Gail Rollins."

She enjoyed the feel of his embrace. "I love you too." The moment ended when Wade was unable to stifle a seemingly endless yawn. Gail stepped away and winked at him. "So the honeymoon is finally over, and hugging me is now boring?"

"Not at all," Wade said as he once again held her close. "Is everything ready for tomorrow?"

"I think so. The stockings are hung on the fireplace, and the milk and cookies are out for Santa."

Wade kissed Gail on the forehead. "Good. So there is a chance."

She watched him pull down the covers and climb into bed. "A chance for what, might I ask?"

He patted the bed beside him and smiled. "I'm looking forward to a good night's sleep."

Gail climbed into bed and turned out the light. She welcomed the prospect of a good sleep before a long Christmas day.

Wade gave another big yawn and said, "I really am surprised at how well the family is getting along. There have only been a couple of times when I thought that we would have to call the police to quell the riots."

Gail hit him with her pillow. They got very little sleep after all because she and Wade talked well into the early hours about everything that had transpired that day.

Gail rose early Christmas morning and went down for a final check on the gifts and the stockings before the rest of the family awoke. As she straightened the candy canes and the other treasures sticking out from the stockings, Gail couldn't help but smile as she remembered the first year that patrolling the stockings on Christmas morning had become necessary. When Dale was six years old, he had gone down early and sifted through all the stockings. Not being happy with what he had received, Dale had loaded his stocking with the good stuff from his siblings' stockings before returning to bed for the agonizing wait for the wakeup call.

Gail chuckled as she recalled just how awkward the moment had been for her parents. They tried to correct the situation but were at a loss to explain how they knew what Santa would have put into each stocking.

Gail enjoyed reliving that and other special memories from Christmases past. Satisfied that everything was in order with the gifts and stockings, Gail was about to return to her room when she was startled by a noise behind her in the darkness. She instinctively reached for the fireplace poker.

"Just like old times, isn't it, sis?"

Gail relaxed as she pulled her hand away from the poker and turned to find Dale fully dressed with his coat on, sitting on the couch.

"What's like old times?" Gail tried to compose herself and hoped that Dale hadn't noticed her reach for the poker.

Dale laughed softly as he motioned for Gail to join him and patted the cushion beside him. "It's just like old times with me coming down early to check things out and you coming down to make sure that I didn't take all the good stuff for myself."

"It's no wonder that Jerry has a hard time trusting you. Every year you would take the best stocking stuffers and leave him with the filler."

Dale chuckled. "And the best part was he couldn't say anything because Mom always said that if there was one complaint about the gifts from Santa, there would be no gifts next year."

Gail placed her hand on his knee. "So what has you up so early, and why are you sitting in the dark with your coat on?"

After a couple of attempts to adjust the coat so that it felt less like a straitjacket, Dale said, "I'm going over to the Mexican embassy this morning."

"You're going to ditch the family again?"

"Relax, sis. I will be back in time to open gifts with the family. The real reason I'm up so early is that I hoped to find some time alone with you so that we could talk in private."

Gail could scarcely conceal her surprise when she asked, "You want to talk with me, alone?"

Even in the subdued light, Gail could see that Dale found humor in her response. "As surprising as that sounds, I do enjoy our time together, and I want to talk to you." He placed his hand on hers. "But since there never seems to be enough time to talk with you during the day, I figured that I might have a chance to talk with you this morning."

"What made you think that I would be up at this time?"

Dale rubbed the back of her hand. "Think about it. I'm in the house, and there are Christmas stockings to raid. I knew you would be down."

Gail stifled the urge to laugh but took the opportunity to state, "If you would have stuck around instead of running off, there would have been lots of time this week to talk."

Dale feigned pulling a dagger from his heart. "Ouch!"

After the moment of levity, she asked, "So what do you want to talk about?"

Dale didn't seem to know where to begin. When he finally spoke, he sounded apologetic. "I wasn't supposed to know about your secret meeting the other night, but I did, and I went."

Gail was surprised that she hadn't seen him but was pleased to know that he cared enough to go.

"I can't stop wondering what you felt when you met your birth mother and whether you still think that it was worth the effort to finally meet her."

Gail was so surprised and touched by Dale's interest in someone other than himself that she was unable to hold back the unexpected tears that surfaced. "Why do you want to know about my feelings after meeting my birth mother?" Gail looked at Dale closely. "Even Mom hasn't asked me about it."

Dale smiled. "Mom really does want to know and is probably waiting until she has time to sit and talk with you alone. If you bring it up, I'm sure that Mom will drop everything to talk with you."

Gail sighed. "You could be right, but she seemed so excited for me before the meeting, and I just assumed that she would ask about it before now." She gave another sigh. "So what exactly do you want to know about my feelings—and why?"

Dale's uncertainty about how to proceed was more obvious than before as he prepared to respond. When he finally spoke again, the words seemed labored. "I'm not so much asking for myself as for Amanda."

Gail saw an opportunity to have some fun at Dale's expense and help him relax. "So Amanda knows about the meeting as well?"

Dale stammered, "No, she doesn't, and if she knew what I am asking you, she would be so embarrassed that she might never speak to me again." He shifted on the couch as if to stand, but Gail stopped him by placing her hand on his knee.

"What is it you want to ask me?"

Dale settled back on the couch. "Since the death of her adoptive parents in a tragic accident, Amanda has been obsessed with trying to locate her birth mother. I feel like I should be more supportive of her efforts, but I don't know what to do." There was a long pause. "I have heard some horror stories about people finding birth mothers who do not wish to be found and how hurtful the rejection can be."

Gail sighed. "So have I, but that never stopped me from looking."

Dale had a serious expression. "I need to know if you felt that the risk of rejection was worth your efforts to meet your birth mother."

It was Gail's turn to hesitate as she considered her answer. "Yes, I feel it most definitely was." Gail was impressed that her seemingly self-centered brother was actually concerned enough about Amanda and what she was going through that he wanted to help. Unfortunately, it seemed that he was willing to help only if the experience would be positive and not cause her more hurt.

As they sat in the darkness of the early morning, the only light was coming from the small night-lights along the hallway, but there was enough illumination for Gail to see the troubled look on his face. Several minutes passed before Dale spoke again. "If it had been you making first contact with your birth mother, and she had rejected you, how do you think you might have felt?"

Gail was silent as she considered this. Many a time, she had considered giving up the quest because she thought that not knowing might be better than being rejected, but deep inside she'd had the feeling that she must keep trying. Gail found her mind wandering but remembered that Dale had asked a question that she knew had to be answered. Dale never asked questions without purpose, and this one seemed personal.

Gail hoped that her answer would provide Dale with what he needed to hear. "There were times that I truly feared what being rejected by my birth mother might do to me." Gail started losing the battle to control her emotions as the clear, firm tone of her voice began to waver. "The prospect of being rejected brought a paralyzing fear as long as I allowed myself to dwell on the negative. Thinking good thoughts is what kept me going, but even those thoughts were fleeting at times."

Dale handed Gail a tissue. "I really don't need to know if it is going to cause you pain."

Gail took the tissue and wiped her tears. "The only time that I felt peace while looking for my birth mother and having thoughts about being rejected was when I realized that whether she loved me or not, I am loved. I have loving parents who adopted me into their family as one of their own, and I have loving brothers." She smiled and took Dale by the hand. "They even come to family reunions when it seems they would rather be on the moon."

Dale said softly, "It's no sacrifice to be with family who love and care for you, even though we don't always see eye to eye."

Gail reached out and gave Dale a hug. "I love you."

Dale embraced Gail. "Love you too, sis."

Gail continued with her answer to Dale's question. "I have a wonderful husband who loves me and has been there for me through good and bad as I've continued my search, and I also have my own children who love me. It's all good."

"So Amanda might get over this obsession with finding her birth mother?"

Finding the right words to say was difficult because she was afraid that Dale would take them the wrong way and think that she was meddling. Gail kept searching for other words that would be more appropriate but couldn't.

"Amanda may get over this obsession but will always yearn to meet her birth mother. She has lost the people in her life that she knows love her."

Dale nodded his head in agreement. "She did take the loss hard."

Gail cleared her throat. "She doesn't realize just how much she is loved, and it doesn't help when the man that she cares deeply about doesn't tell her. You need to tell her that you love her."

Dale looked like a deer in headlights. Gail had expected to be ready to beg forgiveness from her brother at a moment's notice after she had finished speaking. But strangely enough, she was at peace as she waited for Dale to respond.

Dale stood as if to leave. After carefully wrapping his scarf around his neck and closing his coat collar, he fumbled for his gloves and the keys to Wade's car. "You have given me a lot to think about this morning, like I knew you would." Dale started for the door and then turned back. "I have always enjoyed our talks because you have a way of helping me understand. Can I ask a favor of you?"

There was no hesitation. "You certainly may."

Dale looked relieved. "Good. There is this blonde-haired girl who works at the food court."

"And you would like me to check her out for you the way Jerry used to check girls out for you?"

The look on Dale's face was priceless, and it was difficult for Gail to keep from laughing.

Dale regained his composure and then smiled. "Not at all. This young lady appears to be in some emotional distress about adoption and would probably gain a lot from talking with you."

"How would she gain a lot from talking with me?"

"She is unsure of what to expect about finding and meeting her birth mother." As he spoke about his encounter with the girl, there was softness in Dale's eyes that Gail had rarely seen. "She had seen the family hiding in the store windows across from the food court and knew that I belonged from watching my adventure in a store window. She was curious about what was happening."

Hearing this made Gail curious about the nature of his adventure, but she refrained from asking any questions, for now.

Dale continued. "When I told her that the family just wanted to watch the meeting with your birth mother, she said that she could only wonder how her family would react when she found her birth mother."

"I can see how she might wonder. I never knew how my family would react." She smiled. "It felt good to see how far you would go to support, and share the moment. Deep inside me I knew that my family would be there for me."

"Even though, you never told us about the meeting?" Dale lightly nudged her ribs.

"I'm sorry about that, but they had only wanted a small meeting with the four of us." She paused. "On the plus side, my birth mother was relieved to learn that I had been adopted into a wonderful family."

"Boy do we have her fooled." Dale said as he rubbed Gail's hand.

They shared a quiet laugh.

"My birth mother commented about seeing Dad sitting in the display, squinting, while his glasses were sitting on top of his head."

They shared another quiet laugh.

The softness was still visible in Dale's eyes. "You need to go speak with the girl from the food court."

"What makes you say that?"

"Watching the meeting, and our family on display, brought her to tears – and not just a few tears. I really feel that it would help if you would speak with her."

Seeing Dale with so much concern for others was definitely different, but Gail was certain that she could get used to the new Dale. Unsure of what she could say to the girl that would be of any value, or whether the girl would even talk with her, Gail thought for a moment. "How will I know who she is other than her being blonde?"

Dale smiled. "When you walk up to, *The Igloo*, ask for the girl who covered the shortage for a deadbeat customer whose family pretended to be window displays. That should start the conversation nicely."

"*The Igloo* ... got it."

"That's right, and if you order the Christmas special, ask for the penguin ornament so Amber can put it with the polar bear ornament I gave her."

He checked his watch and started for the door, but before leaving, he repeated his promise. "I will be back in time to open gifts with the family."

The door clicked tightly behind Dale. As Gail turned back toward the stockings, she found herself face-to-face with her mother, who was reaching for a hug. They embraced a few moments before her mother said, "I love you so much."

"I love you too." Gail felt a wet patch on her shoulder. "What has you up so early, and why are you crying?"

"I had hoped that you would be down here checking the stockings so we could talk. When I heard you talking with Dale, I chose to stay out of sight."

"Did you hear all of our conversation?" Gail asked, beginning to make sense of her mother's emotional state so early in the morning.

"Not all, but enough." Gail's mother took her by the hand and started toward the stairs. "Christmas morning comes mighty early, so we should try to get some more sleep." At the foot of the stairs, they stopped, and there was another big hug. "Thank you for the best gift a mother could ever ask for."

Christmas Day had finally arrived. With it came relative peace and tranquility because no new incidents between family members had occurred to spoil the moment. So far the only disappointment was that Dale had chosen to leave before the family was awake. Gail and her mother were alone in the kitchen, preparing for breakfast and having a wonderful conversation. Everything her mother wanted to know about the meeting had been discussed, and now they were ready to start cooking.

"So how late do you think Lisa will sleep in today?" Gail asked as she placed a dish in the oven.

Her mother smiled. "Until she smells the food cooking and knows that the bulk of the work has been done." She looked around to make sure they were still alone. "Lisa is quite willing to let others do the work. Last Christmas at her house, she claimed to have a headache every day, and I ended up doing all of the cooking and dishwashing."

Gail did a quick count to make sure there were enough disposable dishes and placed them on the counter so that meals could be dished up buffet-style. "I sure hope Dale returns at a decent time. Once breakfast is over, it will be hard to keep the children from opening their gifts."

"He did promise, and until he is late, he has kept his word."

Hearing those words brought back memories of her youth. Gail remembered the first time her mother had set the alarm clock and placed it in the bathroom. If Gail returned home on time, she would be able to turn off the alarm before it sounded. When she was late, the alarm would wake her mother and guarantee that she was grounded, but only after a stern lecture. "But how will we know he is late? There is no alarm clock in the bathroom."

They shared a laugh. "Sweetheart, you need to learn how to relax more. Things have a way of working out, and worrying over things we can't control doesn't make any difference to the outcome."

Gail admired her mother's wisdom but knew that a little worry was a good thing. She thought about all the incidents that had occurred that could have turned the reunion into a disaster. Once she got past the ruined seafood feast and the scrambling to find the Mexican food replacements, complete with hot peppers, Gail had to concede that worry would not have prevented what had happened. "You're right. You can't control events; you can only control your reactions."

"Exactly. One day you and your family will laugh about the grape drink in the fish tank, the wet bed, and the cold cereal fiasco, along with many other incidents that are the fabric of memories you will always have about this reunion."

It was comforting to think that one day even Jason and Amber would share a laugh over their memories of the reunion.

Just then, Gail heard Brandon cry and heard Lisa blame Amber for being too selfish to share. "Lisa's up!" she said. Gail took a deep breath as her mind was flooded by the memories of how their last reunion had ended. Things had appeared to be going so well, and then disaster had struck. Just as she feared that the worst was going to happen again, cooler heads prevailed, and everything returned to normal. Gail didn't know whether to laugh or scowl when she first entered the family room and saw Wade sitting behind Lisa with the phone in his hand, pretending to dial 911. She remembered the comment Wade had made the night before about not having to call the police to keep the peace. Gail simply looked away. "Breakfast is ready."

Gail had the sinking feeling that in spite of his promise and best intentions, Dale was going to miss Christmas morning with the family. Stalling to give Dale time to return for the gift exchange, Gail and her mother tried to keep the family busy with breakfast. When the final disposable plate was thrown in the garbage bag, Gail tied it closed. "Mom, I can't believe how smoothly breakfast went this morning. Even the children had one choice of cold cereal and actually liked it."

"That is part of the magic Christmas morning brings when it comes to little children." Gail's mother returned a dish towel to the rack. "They even seem to be better behaved until after the gifts are opened."

Amber and Brandon were now being extremely well behaved, holding hands when they went to sit in front of the mountain of gifts. It had been hours since Dale left, and he should have been back by now, Gail thought. As the last of the pots was placed into the cupboard, Gail asked her mother, "So how much longer do you think the kids will be willing to wait before they open gifts?"

She didn't have to wonder long because Brandon began crying a moment later, and Amber came running up to her with a small package in her hand. The wrapping paper was torn and barely concealed the treasure inside. "Aunt Lisa gave Brandon a present to open before we are supposed to."

Gail gave Amber a hug. "It's all right if he opens it. His mother gave it to him to open."

Amber returned the gift to Brandon, who took it with a squeal of delight and ran to stand behind his mother.

The beeping and whirring of the small electronic toy told everyone that Brandon had been successful in opening his small gift, and his squeals of excitement made it difficult to keep Amber from wanting to open one.

She crawled out from under the tree with one of her gifts. "Can I open a present now?"

Gail checked the tag. It was to Amber from Dale. "You need to wait until Uncle Dale is here to open his gift to you. He wanted to be here when you open it."

Amber went under the tree a second time and found the gift from her grandparents. She avoided Gail and sat on the couch between them. "Can I please open this present from Grandma and Grandpa?"

Ready or not, Gail knew that the time to open gifts had arrived. She nodded her approval, and Amber carefully exposed the gift without making a single tear in the paper. Amber protested mildly whenever her grandma tried to help. Once the wrapping paper was removed, she opened the box to reveal the doll she had requested for Christmas. Amber squealed with delight and gave big hugs and kisses to her grandparents. She then presented the box to her grandma. "Can you please help me get the doll out of the box?"

"I would love to." Her grandma took the box and began to remove the ties that secured the doll.

The front door opened and closed before either child could request another gift to open. Gail was relieved that Dale had been true to his word and returned as promised. The room became silent, except for the sound of Brandon's toy, when Dale entered the room. He stepped aside to allow the attractive young lady with him to enter. "I would like you to meet a very dear friend of mine, Consuela Gonzales." He waited for the family to respond. "She wanted to meet the family that I kept leaving her to be with all week, so I brought her with me."

Gail crossed the room. "Please let me take your coat."

"Thank you." Consuela handed her scarf and coat to Gail.

Gail hadn't noticed Consuela's ring at first but definitely became aware of it when the large diamond scratched her hand. "I am so happy to welcome you into our home, and we are glad that you could join us." Gail took their coats and showed them a place to sit.

When Gail returned to the room, Amber was standing in front of Dale and Consuela with her most angelic look. "Uncle Dale, can I please open the gift you bought me?"

"Is it time to open gifts?"

Amber held up her new doll. "See what Grandma and Grandpa gave me?"

"If it is time to open gifts, you may open the one from me."

Gail nodded her approval, and Amber gave a squeal of delight as she rushed across the room to retrieve the gift. She returned to sit on Dale's lap and then proceeded to tear the wrapping paper from the gift. There was another squeal of delight when she opened the box and found another of the items she had requested for Christmas.

Amber turned to Consuela. "Could you help me get the toy from the box?"

As Consuela worked to free the toy, Amber reached out to touch the ring. "Did Uncle Dale give you that ring? Can I see it?"

Consuela was gracious and held the ring at different angles for Amber and those sitting close to see. Amber looked as if she was going to ask another question but never got the chance.

"Son, is there something that you forgot to tell us?" Grandma asked.

Gail could tell that Dale was going to have some fun with the situation and cringed when he replied, "I can't think of anything."

Lisa joined in. "Is that or is that not an engagement ring on Consuela's hand?"

Dale took Consuela's hand and examined the ring. "It appears that the ring on her finger is an engagement ring. And it is a very nice engagement ring."

Gail could sense the growing frustration with Dale and his evasive answers. It was obvious that her mother and Lisa were tired of playing twenty questions. She realized that not everyone in the room was familiar with the wedding that had never been. "How are your parents doing since you called off the wedding?"

Consuela looked surprise as she glanced at Dale and then back at Gail. "My father is disappointed, as you can imagine, because he is really fond of Ramón, and he is from a very well-respected family."

"How is your mother doing?"

"My mother is doing well. She was disappointed at first but respects my decision."

Amber took the gift box from Consuela, who had stopped trying to remove the tie wraps when Amber had asked her about the ring. Amber then looked at Consuela with the thoughtful expression that appeared whenever there were questions in her pretty little head that needed to be answered. "Does your mother like Uncle Dale?"

"Yes, she does," Consuela said being courteous to the little girl in front of her.

"Does she greet him at the door with a hug and kiss?"

Gail could tell that Consuela was at a loss for words as she tried to understand the reasoning behind the question, so Gail spoke up. "Why would you want to know that, Amber?"

Amber looked pleased with herself when she responded. "If one person likes another person a lot, they greet them with a hug and kiss at the door like Jason greeted Vicki when she came to the house. So if your mother likes Uncle Dale a lot, she should greet him with a hug and kiss. So does she?"

Consuela gave a small laugh. "No, she doesn't greet him with a hug and kiss when he comes." She must have thought that her answer would be enough to satisfy Amber, but she soon realized her mistake.

Amber had a serious look when she asked, "Do you like Uncle Dale enough to greet him with a hug and a kiss?"

A blush came to Consuela's face, and Gail knew that something had to be done to distract her daughter. "Amber, can you help me give everyone their gifts to open?"

When Amber failed to look away from Consuela, it was obvious that she wanted an answer. Amber wasn't the only one awaiting an answer; Lisa was ignoring Brandon, with her attention focused on Consuela.

"I have greeted Dale at times with a hug."

"And have you greeted him with a kiss?" Amber placed her hands on her hips.

Consuela smiled and took Amber by the hand. "I have greeted Dale with both a hug and a kiss when he has come to visit me. I greet a lot of people that way." Consuela pulled Amber close to give her a hug and a kiss on the cheek. "That is how we greet people in my country."

Gail repeated her request. "Amber, can you please help me with the gifts? You are the right size to find the gifts behind the tree."

When all of the gifts had been opened and the children were playing with their newfound treasures, Gail invited Dale and Consuela to help her in the kitchen. Before any conversation could begin, the kitchen was full of helpers—helpers who were more eager to hear what might be said than they were to prepare the meal. Once all the helpers had a task to perform, there was nothing left for Gail, Dale, and Consuela to do, and eventually, they left the kitchen.

In the hallway they were met by a determined-looking little girl. Amber stood with her hands on her hips and an expression that meant there were questions—and most likely a lot of them—as she stared down her uncle. Dale knelt down and soon regretted it.

"Where are the pajamas you bought me?"

Dale looked puzzled. "I never bought you any pajamas."

"Yes, you did." Amber folded her arms and gave a big sigh of disgust. "You bought a pair of red pajamas."

"Who told you that?"

"Jason said that Vicki told him that you bought some pretty red pajamas for a special girl." Amber began to tap her foot.

"Jason told you that?"

"Yes, and you always say that I am your special girl. So where are they?"

Dale smiled as he looked at the anticipation in Jason's eyes. "I think Jason and Vicki played a trick on you. You already opened the gift I bought you."

Amber looked back at Jason. "Jerk!"

"Amber, that isn't a very nice thing to call your brother," Gail said as she hugged Amber. "Say you're sorry."

"No. He is a jerk for saying that," Amber said as she went to play.

Gail was impressed at how quickly Dale had come up with an answer that seemed to satisfy Amber. Amber may have been satisfied, but Gail was definitely going to ask Dale about the pajamas later.

The hallway was not designed to hold a lot of people, but suddenly, the whole family was there, plus Consuela. Gail resigned herself to having to wait to speak with Dale and herded the family back to the living room. After a pleasant visit, Dale and Consuela excused themselves.

As Dale slipped past Gail, he whispered, "I'm going to rummage through Christmas stockings in the morning. Care to join me?"

Gail laughed. "It's a date."

As Gail closed the door behind Dale and Consuela, she detected a burning smell coming from the kitchen. She rushed past the entire family to see what her helpers had done to their Christmas dinner.

The damage was minimal because only one pot of vegetables had made it to the stove, but they were ruined because the pot had boiled dry. As for the rest of the meal, each dish had been abandoned at various degrees of preparation, and the kitchen looked as if an evacuation order had been issued. It appeared that everyone had dropped what they were doing once she had left the kitchen with Dale and Consuela.

Wade joined Gail in the kitchen as she began to get the meal back on track. "This family deserves to have another meal of Mexican food," Gail muttered as she tossed not only the burnt vegetables but also the ruined pot into the garbage. Soon the rest of the food was cooking and complimenting the aroma of the turkey that filled the air. The wonderful aroma prompted inquiries from those who had fled the kitchen about when dinner would be ready.

While Wade and Gail tended to the meal, it would have been the perfect time to speak about her early-morning conversations, except for the number of interruptions from family who wanted to loiter and listen, but not actually help with the meal. When Lisa made a third visit to the kitchen,

Gail handed her a stack of plates. "Go set the table. We are almost ready to eat."

After the meal all the dishes were cleared from the table, and Gail was alone in the kitchen while family congregated in the living room. Gail was disappointed that she was being taken for granted as the family took advantage of her hospitality and left her to clean up again. She wanted to discuss the prospects of a spring destination wedding in Mexico for Dale and Consuela as much as the next person. She knew that the mess would wait until later and that she could join the others, but she didn't. She knew who would get stuck doing it, so she might as well get it over with.

Gail filled the sink with warm soapy water and turned off the faucet. She surveyed the stacks of dishes and was about to throw down the dishrag in disgust when she had an idea. Gail checked to make sure that she was alone. She reached for her cell phone, dialed a number, and placed the phone in a basket under the dirty towels. Soon her house phone rang; she let it ring twice and then answered it loud enough to be heard by the family.

"Dale, I didn't expect to hear from you until tonight." Before the next words could leave her lips, the kitchen became a hub of activity as once again the helpers arrived to do the dishes so that they could justify listening to the conversation.

"What do I think of Jamaica as a destination?" Gail paused as she dried another dish and handed it to Lisa. "A person would definitely have some breathtaking background for their wedding pictures. In fact, there were two wedding parties at the base of the falls when we went."

Gail found it difficult to move as there was hardly any room, her mother stood close on one side, and Lisa was even closer on the other side.

"Hawaii? I could force myself to attend a wedding there, if I had to." Gail covered the mouthpiece of the phone and looked at Lisa. "What do you think of Hawaii as a wedding destination?"

Lisa smiled. "I know the perfect place on Maui, and I think we could get a great deal from our time-share for the family."

Gail turned her attention back to the phone. "Did I hear you right? Did you just ask what I thought about Alaska at Christmas?"

Gail's mother and Lisa both stood back and shook their heads, while waving their hands in front of them.

"I don't think the family would like Alaska in the winter. I'm sure it is pretty, but that white stuff on the ground isn't sand." Gail covered the phone again. "He's asking what you think of the Mayan Riviera in July."

The dishes were almost done when Gail said, "We will discuss the options you have given, and let you know what we think. Just remember that the memories of that day will be yours forever." She paused. "Love you to."

Gail hung up the phone and Lisa immediately asked, "Dale was joking about Alaska, right?"

"You heard as much as I did. When I know more, I will be sure to share with you." When Gail was the last person left in the spotless kitchen, she tossed the dish towel into the basket, retrieved the cell phone, and placed it back on the charger.

When Dale arrived later that evening, he was at a loss as to the earlier phone call his mother and Lisa were talking about. He looked to Gail, who winked at him and smiled as she played with one of the Christmas stockings hanging on the mantel.

Gail was relieved that Dale knew enough to play along. Dale yawned and stretched. "It's late, and I'm beat. I hope you don't mind but I'm going to bed," He forced another yawn. "I'll see you fine people in the morning." There was a smile on his face as he winked at Gail and heard another round of speculation begin about his relationship with Consuela.

Chapter Ten

EARLY THE NEXT MORNING, Gail found Dale arranging some items in the two stockings hanging on the mantel.

"Busted!" Dale joked as he took the stockings and handed one to Gail.

They sat on the couch, and Gail was surprised at the amount of stuffers that Dale had put in the stockings as she checked the contents. She removed the wrapper from a chocolate mint stick. "I wonder what the kids would say about eating chocolate before breakfast." She smiled and downed it in a single bite.

"So what is this phone call that I allegedly made to you after dinner?" Dale asked as he started to suck on the end of a candy cane. "It certainly has Mom and Lisa all excited."

Gail smiled. "I figured it would when I made the call." She proceeded to tell Dale all the details about the call and could tell by his smile that he approved.

"I always knew that you were resourceful, but I'm impressed that you found a way to tap into Mom's and Lisa's curiosity about me in order to have them help with the dishes." Dale pretended to bow down to her.

Gail acknowledged his gesture. "Now let's be sure that you have your facts right."

"Absolutely, so my first destination choice was Jamaica?"

"Yes, the waterfall was appealing to you as a background for your wedding pictures."

"Got it, and Hawaii?"

Gail smiled. "Lisa had commented on Maui, and how they might score a deal for the family in their time-share."

Dale rubbed his chin. "That sounds promising; do you think the offer will still be there if she discovers the truth about the phone call?"

"No comment." Gail said, as they shared a quiet laugh. "Next was the option of Alaska during the winter, to be exact, at Christmas."

Just the thought of all that crisp fresh air made Dale shiver. "That was cruel, but then again, the Mayan Riviera during July might be just as cruel."

Dale reviewed the main points until Gail was confident that his story would be consistent to the tantalizing tidbits she had laid down as bait.

The prospect of playing along must have appealed to Dale because he was wearing a large smile when he turned to Gail. "This is going to be great." He rubbed his hands in anticipation and then became more serious. "I believe that I owe you an explanation about the ring on Consuela's finger."

Gail gave a barely perceptible nod. "Yes, you do. You were just lucky that Amber was distracted by the prospect of opening gifts when she asked about the ring." She paused. "I'm curious to see the pajamas she thought she was getting."

"There were no pajamas." Dale was quite emphatic in his denial. "As for the ring on Consuela's finger, it is definitely an engagement ring."

Gail sensed he was being evasive, so she was more direct with her question. "Did you give Consuela a ring?"

Dale became more reserved. "Consuela's fiancé gave her the ring."

Gail said in a monotone voice, "I figured as much. Who else but her fiancé would give her an engagement ring? The big question is, who is the fiancé?" She stared at Dale.

Dale appeared disappointed as he answered the question. "Ramón is still lucky enough to be called her fiancé. But only if he gets his act together."

It had been obvious to Gail how much Consuela meant to Dale when they were at the house the day before. She had also noticed how much Consuela cared for Dale. "So what raging river, burning desert, or tallest mountain does this man have to cross to regain her affections?"

Gail gave Dale a moment to think about what she had said. He was emotional and spoke in a near whisper. "Consuela told me that she still loves Ramón and is willing to help him understand how important marriage is to her and in time forgive him if he is sincere."

Gail refrained from saying what she was thinking and cleared her throat. "How is she going to know when he is sincere?"

"I don't know." Dale shook his head subtly from side to side.

"The more important question might be, are you planning to wait until Consuela makes a decision on Ramón before you get on with your own life?"

Dale shrugged his shoulders. "I'm not sure. I might wait for a little while."

Gail smacked the back of his head. "Amanda is not going to wait forever. By the time Consuela makes a decision about Ramón, you may have lost both of them."

Dale rubbed the back of his head. "Ouch."

"Good, I'm glad you felt it. At least part of your brain is working."

Dale continued to rub the back of his head. "Consuela is a deep thinker. I'm not sure what she is expecting from Ramón, but I do know that she is willing to give him another chance."

"I wouldn't give him another chance to hurt me." Gail moved her hand and noticed Dale duck. "Does she have a plan at least?"

Dale moved Gail's hand from his shoulder to her lap. "I think that she has a plan. After I told Consuela something

Amanda had told me, she got excited and repeated some saying her mother always says."

"And what saying might that be?"

Dale was silent for a few seconds, seemingly reciting the phrase in his head. When he appeared satisfied with his recollection, he said, "In the eyes of man, it requires torrents of blood to erase our faults, yet in the eyes of God, a single sincere tear will suffice." He paused a moment. "At least I think it went something like that."

Gail was impressed by the wisdom of those words. At times when she remembered things that had been done to her, she thought that even torrents of blood wouldn't be enough to erase the memories and feelings. Gail thought about how she felt toward those who had wronged her. She was curious about Consuela's change of heart. "So what did you repeat from Amanda that would make Consuela decide to forgive, considering how she put the run on Ramón and the bridesmaids?

Dale took a deep breath. "Let me tell you the story as it actually happened and not Angelo's interpretation."

"That works for me." Gail smiled. "Is the truth just as juicy as Angelo's version?"

Dale rolled his eyes. "I'll let you keep Angelo's version of what had happened before I arrived. It's close enough to the truth to let it stand."

"So what happened after you arrived?"

Dale spoke softly. "When I first arrived at the embassy, the only person Consuela was willing to speak with was me. Consuela was so upset that she wasn't even willing to speak with her mother."

"She wouldn't even talk to her own mother?"

"Not at all. It seems that her mother might love Ramón more than Consuela does. She was really upset with Consuela when Ramón was sent packing."

"Awkward."

"No kidding. Anyway, once I had entered the room and the door had closed behind me, I saw this beautiful young lady sitting on the edge of her bed. Consuela's chin was resting on her hands as she looked off into the distance." Dale described the scene and how visible her pain was. "When I was close enough, she stood only long enough to fall into my arms and cry." Dale was noticeably touched as he repeated himself a few times. "She just stood in my arms, sobbing."

Gail could visualize the scene and could even relate to some of the emotions that Consuela would have been feeling. Wade had never caused a situation like this, but over the years she had experienced her share of emotional pain. It was all Gail could do to keep her emotions in check as Dale told the story.

"I spent the better part of that evening alone with Consuela, just letting her talk."

As Gail listened to the story, she thought about this lovely young lady who had been disappointed and hurt by the man who had asked her to marry him and had promised to love and protect her. Gail could feel her contempt for the man building as she wondered what pain and emotional hurt was in store for her daughter at the hands of the men of this world. Realizing that her mind had wandered while Dale was talking, she snapped back to the conversation and had to stop him and ask him some questions.

"So when you were talking and Consuela asked you what marriage meant to you, you said what?" Gail wanted to be sure that she had heard and understood him correctly.

"I told her that marriage was very important to me, and when I marry, I intend to marry the girl of my dreams who will also be my best friend. I intend to marry her forever. None of this until-death-do-us-part nonsense."

Gail nodded her head. "That's what I thought you said. So how did Consuela respond?"

Dale laughed. "About the same as you. She asked me to stop and repeat myself, only I think she did it for a different reason."

They shared a subdued chuckle. "You're probably right. I never expected to hear words like that, from my brother. So how did you come up with that answer?"

"I'm no deep thinker when it comes to this sort of thing, but Amanda's mother was. Just before the accident that took her parents, they spoke with Amanda about marriage and family."

"Her parents were tired of waiting for you to propose to their daughter and decided to give her some advice, huh?"

Dale gave her a look that made her laugh. "It's possible, but I think the insight had more to do with her father's recent health issues. They had been giving a lot of thought to how unfair it seemed that their marriage would end at death."

There was no laughter or smart remark from Gail. Many times she had found herself thinking that very thought. "So what advice did Amanda receive?"

"I'm not sure what they told her, but it changed the way Amanda was looking at marriage. I heard her talking with one the girls at work about it, and I don't think she knew I could hear them."

Gail sensed that Dale was uncomfortable by the way he played with the armrest cover. She was curious about what Amanda had said and was afraid that if this moment was lost, she might never know. It was getting light out, and she had heard the sound of a door closing softly. "What did Amanda say?"

Dale flattened the corner of the armrest cover. "Amanda said that the man she marries must be willing to love her forever, not simply until death should they part or until he tires of her. It has to be forever."

"Are you intimidated by the standard Amanda has set?"

"Maybe I am just a little intimidated. It is a lot higher than her old standard of a good personality and being good friends."

Gail rubbed Dale's knee. "Amanda is no different from most women. Marriage is a big deal. When a woman opens her heart to a man, she does not want it broken."

"I realize this." Dale scratched behind his ear and went silent. A second door opened and closed upstairs. "It seems sad to think that marriage ends at death. With marriage being ordained by God, why would he make us sad by ending marriage at death?"

A toilet flushed, and another door closed. Gail had a multitude of questions forming in her mind but no answer for her brother that seemed appropriate. With the sound of feet on the stairs, she knew the conversation was over. "Aren't you glad that Amber didn't ask you that question?"

"No kidding."

Gail loaded the stuffers back into the stockings. In an attempt to clarify in her mind what Dale's position was, she asked, "So if Ramón isn't willing to commit to Consuela forever, they're done, and you can move in?"

Dale looked at his watch. "I'll answer that question after I call Amanda and wish my very good friend a belated Merry Christmas." He hugged Gail. "Thank you."

"You're welcome, and I hope you find the answer you are looking for."

"Thanks to you, I think I already know the answer." Dale left for the den as he heard voices at the top of the stairs. Gail knew that Dale wanted to be out of sight before his mother and Lisa started to question him about Consuela.

Gail took a deep breath when she heard Lisa ask, "Is Gail getting breakfast ready? Brandon is hungry."

Chapter Eleven

THE HOUSE WAS A hub of activity, and Gail had things under control. Amber and Brandon had finished breakfast and were quite content to play with their new toys. The only ones not at peace seemed to be her mother and Lisa, who kept looking for Dale.

On several occasions Gail had been asked if she was feeling well. When Jason asked if she was feeling well, Gail took him to the side. "So why do you think that I'm not feeling well?"

Jason smiled. "You never wear your pajamas and housecoat for extended periods unless you are sick."

Gail looked at her attire and laughed. "I forgot that I never went up to change."

Wade joined the conversation. "It probably doesn't help that you look tired because of your early-morning visits with Dale."

Gail countered, "I'm sure the late-night visits with you aren't helping much either."

Wade looked in the mirror and rubbed his face. "Do I have bags forming under my eyes?"

Just then Amber entered the room. "Mommy, is that the bag you were talking about the other morning?"

"No, sweetheart."

Amber looked at Gail. "Are you feeling sick?"

"Why do you ask?"

"Both Grandma and Lisa are talking about you still being in your pajamas."

Wade took Amber in his arms. "Do you think that Mom should get dressed?"

"Yes. She told me that I had to."

Wade waited until Amber had finished giving Gail the look. "What do you think Mrs. Tennant would think if she were to stop by and see your mother still in her pajamas?"

"She would think that Mommy was sick."

"What do you think Mrs. Tennant would do if she thought Mommy was sick?"

Gail didn't want to hear the answer. Mrs. Tennant was the leader of the ladies' group at church. If she thought that Gail was sick, there would be more soups and casseroles delivered than they could eat and quite possibly a portion of Mrs. Tennant's "cure." The very thought of that smelly concoction in her house made Gail shudder. "I'll go change. We have no more room for leftovers."

Gail thought about taking a shower, but after Jason and Lisa had finished theirs, she wasn't going to be the one experiencing the sudden shot of cold water at the end. She changed her clothes and applied some makeup before rejoining the family. This was the first time in weeks that Gail had allowed herself to relax, but she was still attentive to potential warning signs.

When Dale emerged from the den, he looked preoccupied but still seemed to notice Lisa moving toward him like a jungle cat stalking her prey. Dale took a path that avoided Lisa. He passed by Gail and grabbed his coat. "We will talk later, but right now I have to leave."

The door shut behind Dale, leaving Gail to wonder what was happening. Lisa joined her and sounded annoyed as they both faced the closed door. "Where is he going? He still hasn't told us when he and Consuela are getting married so we can make plans. Jerry and I have to leave soon, and it would be nice to know these things."

Hearing those words reminded Gail that the reunion was over, and the family would soon be off to their own corners of the world. "He said that he had to leave."

Lisa still sounded annoyed. "He will probably be back once he sees our car pull away."

Gail wouldn't have blamed Dale if that was his reason for leaving, but she felt there was something more. Standing alone by the door and listening to the family made her glad that she had brought the family together for Christmas, and she reminisced over the events of the past few days. Although the reunion had started like an accident looking for a place to happen, she felt that this time together had been worth every awkward moment. Gail had to admit that a few unfortunate incidents had occurred along the way, but she was pleased to see her family closer than when they first arrived.

Dale returned a few hours later. Gail observed how he was acting and asked, "Is there something wrong?"

"Why do you ask?"

"You seem distracted."

Dale smiled. "I am distracted. I'm trying to think of a way to not offend Lisa when I don't answer those questions she is going to ask about Consuela and me."

"She will just have to understand that there is nothing to tell." Gail patted his knee. "It would have been easier to have nothing to tell if you had waited until after they left to bring Consuela by."

"True, but then she wouldn't have met Jerry."

Gail sensed that her brothers were closer than appearances indicated, and she seized the moment to ask a question she had wanted to ask for a long time. "Why do you choose to accept assignments on the other side of the world?"

"It's part of my job."

"But it seems as if you are trying to avoid family by taking those assignments."

Dale looked disappointed. "I thought that if anyone would understand what I am doing, it would be you."

Gail was puzzled by his response. "Understand what?"

"That I take these assignments to be close to family." Her confused expression must have been humorous because Dale smiled as he tried to explain. "I am responsible for those people like Jerry who choose to work overseas, even if they don't like my help. The posting I have allows me to be there for Jerry when things go wrong."

"I never thought about it that way." She paused. "Is it really that dangerous for Jerry?"

Dale related some experiences the two of them had shared where their lives had been in danger because of Jerry's work. After listening to the stories, she was glad that Dale had been there for their brother. With this new insight into the relationship between her brothers, it was now making sense to Gail why at times the brothers seemed to hate each other and at other times seemed like the best of friends. Dale's job was a pain to those in Jerry's position, and Jerry's job caused more work and worry for Dale when there was unrest, which Dale claimed was a constant state of being.

Gail was fairly certain that these stories Dale had told her were still a secret between brothers. "You've never told Mom any of this, have you?"

"No. She would only worry for us all the more and nag us to come home."

The peace and tranquility in the other room seemed to be at risk when Amber voiced her displeasure about something, followed by Lisa saying it wasn't Brandon's fault. Before leaving to run interference, Gail gave her brother a hug. "I'm glad we had this talk. Your secret is safe. Mom will never hear about it from me."

Later in the day, Gail found time to speak with Jerry. When Jerry realized that Gail understood what the relationship was between her brothers, he opened up to her and shared his views on what it was like having Dale looking over his shoulder all the time. "Dale can be a royal pain in the you-know-what at times. That being said, we are all grateful for the times that Dale has gone the extra mile to ensure our safety, even going so far as to put his own life at risk."

"How did he put his life at risk?"

Jerry went thoughtful like he always did when uncertain about whether he should say something. "Do you know how Dale got his limp?"

Gail was curious at this question because she thought she already knew the answer. "Didn't he hurt himself playing sports?"

Jerry smiled. "That's what he would like you to think. The truth of the matter is that he got hurt making us leave our compound and come to the embassy."

"What happened?"

"We didn't think that the situation was as serious as he had told us, and we were willing to wait it out in the compound. Dale drove out and insisted we leave at once." Jerry stopped to dry a tear. "Most of us gave in and left with Dale; others didn't." The next pause was even longer. "On the way back to the embassy, a roadside bomb went off, and some of the shrapnel came through the door and hit Dale's leg."

Gail was shocked to hear this story. "Was he justified in coming to get you?"

Jerry looked uncomfortable as he continued. "Yes, he was justified in his concern. Some of the others who stayed behind are still being held as hostages."

The story saddened Gail, but at the same time she was pleased to see how some things hadn't changed. Her brothers might have fought like cats and dogs growing up, but they always looked out for each other. Even these grown-up adventures came with a familiar expression from their youth: "Don't tell Mom."

After visiting with her brothers, Gail acknowledged that some secrets were better left untold for obvious reasons, and most of them would probably go to the grave without being revealed. She thought about her family and could only imagine the number of things her own children would decide to keep from her so she wouldn't worry. At that same moment she began to worry even more.

Gail was surprised when Wade sat beside her and placed his arm around her. "You look mighty thoughtful in here by yourself when the house is full of family. Have you had enough family togetherness to last for a while?"

"No," Gail said as she nudged him in the ribs. "You can never have too much time with those you love."

"I beg to differ when one of them is Lisa, but I know what you mean."

Another nudge in the ribs brought a brief moment of shared laughter. "That girl can be trying at times," Gail admitted.

Wade pulled Gail close and kissed her cheek. "So what are you thinking about?"

"Things."

"What kind of things?"

"Things like how glad I am that we told my parents about the meeting with my birth mother."

Wade raised an eyebrow. "Even after they violated your trust and told the rest of the family?"

Gail paused to reflect on the events of that evening. "Even after the family showed how much they love and care for me by wanting to share my special moment."

Gail watched Jason helping his grandmother with the latest electronic gadget she had received for Christmas, which no one else seemed to understand how to work. She remembered Jason's act of rebellion in which he had come face-to-face with Vicki, dressed in the last thing in the world that he would have wanted her to see him in. Gail smiled to herself as she thought about the laughs that memory would bring, especially at a wedding reception.

Wade interrupted her thoughts. "So how has the reunion been for you?"

"Why do you ask?"

"You felt that the reunion might bring answers to your prayers. The meeting with your birth mother wasn't a result of the reunion, so can the reunion be considered an answer to a prayer?"

Gail thought a moment. "I am going to say yes."

"In what way is it an answer?"

Gail pointed to the children playing and then at the adults visiting and enjoying each other's company. "It helped bring the family closer."

When Amber left the table and sat in the chair next to the dog family, Gail's mood became more sober. Amber once again began playing with the frayed end of the ribbon where the small puppy should be. Since Amber first became aware of the missing puppy, Gail had searched for an answer to help Amber realize that the puppy was gone. She wanted to explain that even if the puppy never returned, the dog family would be okay.

It was then that Gail realized that she couldn't find the answer because she herself had not wanted to accept that the puppy would never come home. A lump began to form in her throat, and a tear formed in the corner of her eye. Gail scolded herself for being so emotional about something she had no control over. After all, it was an insignificant puppy from an ornament.

Wade interrupted the moment. "What are you thinking about?"

"Nothing. I'm not thinking about anything."

"Then why are there tears?"

Gail didn't want Wade to know what she was emotional about, so she snuggled close to him. "The family won't always be together like this, will we?" Gail took Wade's hand in hers and played with the ring on his finger.

"No, but we will always cherish our memories of times like this."

Gail wiped a tear from her eye. "You're right. We will always have these cherished memories."

Chapter Twelve

THE HOUSE WAS STRANGELY quiet compared to how noisy it had been the previous week with all the laughter and those precarious bonding moments. Dale was still in town, but may as well be gone, since his days were spent with Consuela at the embassy. Right now the loudest noise in the house was the industrial steam cleaner as Gail tried to remove the purple stain from the white rug in front of Amber's fish tank. "Out, out, foul spot," Gail muttered when the stain appeared to be just as bright as it had been before she started cleaning it.

After the new cleaner failed to make the stains magically fade away, she decided to try scrubbing with the hand brush. As she knelt down, her wet pants clung to her legs and pulled tight. The well-worn knees tore open just as the material below the back pockets ripped too. When she shifted to check the damage, the inseams split from the knee to the crotch.

Jason entered the room at that precise moment and couldn't contain his laughter when he saw the condition of the pants. "I wish I had a camera. Your pants make my boarding pants look like new."

Gail turned to Jason and saw him in near fits of hysterical laughter.

Jason tried to catch his breath. "And you said my pants were worn out and should be thrown away."

Gail stood up and looked at herself in the mirror. The reflection she saw was priceless. The cuffs had slid up her calves almost to the knees, and this allowed the material from the upper legs to billow out from the open inseams like a cross between riding pants and sailboat sails. When Jason returned to take a picture, Gail wrapped herself in Amber's quilt and pointed to the door. "You may leave!"

Jason laughed. "You really should change your clothes; you never know who could come to the door. Could you imagine what Mrs. Tennant would do if she saw you dressed like that?"

"I would rather not think about that."

Jason got his picture of the pants and rushed from the room. A moment later, he stuck his head back into the room and took another picture. "Mrs. Tennant would take one look at you, start a clothing drive, and then start taking donations."

Gail shook her head and started to laugh. "Mrs. Tennant is a sweetheart who has the best interests of others in mind, but she can be a little overexuberant."

"Mrs. Tennant can be a lot overexuberant, Mom, especially when you look like a homeless person."

Gail took another look in the mirror. "You're right. I do look like a homeless person who needs a hot shower and a change of clothes." She rubbed her hand over the faded stain. "Right after I finish cleaning the rug. Then the pants go into the rag bin."

No sooner had she finished a final pass with the steam cleaner than Amber came into the room and laughed at the sight of her mother. "You have company."

A small panic attack came and went as Gail contemplated how she was going to move from Amber's room to her own without being seen. The door to Amber's room was visible from the front entry. Gail pulled the large handmade quilt from the bed, but instead of wrapping herself in it, which would be much too obvious, she held it in her arms like a bundle of laundry that draped to the floor. As Gail moved from Amber's room, she didn't see anyone in the front entry, so she figured that her company was already waiting in the family room.

In record time she had changed her clothes and run a comb through her hair in an attempt to look more presentable. Gail arrived downstairs to find Jason and Amber on the couch, laughing.

"Where is my company?" Gail asked as she looked around the room.

Amber was the first to stop laughing long enough to say, "There is no one here. We tricked you."

Gail looked at her loving children sitting together and enjoying the moment in a way that had been missing when the house was full of family. It was nice to hear the laughter, but she was curious as to why they felt they needed to pull this trick on her when she was busy cleaning the house.

"That was quite the trick you pulled," Gail said as she looked toward Jason, who was still giggling.

His was a smile of contentment. "Your hair is almost in place and definitely better-looking than when you were scrubbing the carpet. The dress slacks look nice but don't match that oversized T-shirt from your last cruise." He pointed at her feet. "I'm disappointed that the socks are not even the right color for the rest of the outfit." Jason enjoyed the moment a while longer. "We're still not even."

"Not even for what?" Gail asked as she cocked her head to the side and looked intently at Jason, as if willing him to offer an explanation.

"We're still not even for you not telling me that Vicki was coming to deliver the food before Christmas. We are definitely not even for you allowing me to answer the door in those stupid worn and torn clothes that I had put on to annoy you." Jason folded his arms and scowled. "I thought this might give you an idea of how bad it felt for me to be inappropriately dressed for company."

Perspective was a strange thing because Gail distinctly remembered telling Jason to change his clothes, but in hindsight she could see that things might have been different had she told him who was coming. Gail was about to plead her case but thought better of it and chuckled. "You sure got me good."

Gail shared another laugh with the children and then wanted to clean herself up for the day. It was almost lunchtime, so she said, "Jason, make some lunch for your sister while I have a shower."

"Why do I have to make lunch? There is nothing good to eat."

The look of defiance told Gail that Jason didn't want to make the lunch and was willing to push as far as possible before giving in to the request. "Don't tell me there is nothing good to eat. The freezers are full of meals we never used for the reunion." She listened to a few more feeble excuses and started to lose her patience with such a simple situation. "If I have to make the lunch, you will be eating Mexican food until the last morsel is finished, even the peppers."

Amber started to push Jason toward the kitchen. "You can help me make lunch. I don't want any Mexican food."

Gail smiled at the sight. "Thank you, Amber."

Once Gail had showered and finished her makeup, she dressed as if she was expecting company. She came downstairs to find that Wade, who had decided to work from home today, was still in the den behind closed doors and that her kitchen was a small disaster. Jason had helped Amber make lunch, but they hadn't cleaned up. Gail chose to ignore the kitchen and give Jason a chance to clean the mess. She knew it wouldn't happen before she couldn't wait any longer and cleaned it herself, but she could always hope. Right now her top priority was putting Christmas away for another year.

Gail made good time putting away most of the seasonal decorations, pausing only to finish the last of the stuffers that Dale had placed in her stocking. Once the tree and the ornaments had been carefully placed in boxes, Gail began to pack up the smaller ornaments and decorations. Amber kept interrupting her because she wanted certain decorations left out for just a while longer, including the dog family, which Gail wanted to put away. It seemed that every time she reached for the dogs, Amber would enter the room.

"Mommy, I told you to leave them out," Amber said as she took the decoration from the box.

"Sweetheart, we need to put the decorations away so we can clean the house."

Amber held the dogs close to her heart. "Can we put them in my room?"

* * * * *

While Gail was dealing with the frustration of Amber stopping progress by insisting that the dog family stay out of the box, Wade had his own frustration to deal with.

Wade had taken the day off and was in the den making phone calls. He was becoming increasingly frustrated with his investigator friend as they discussed the information from the papers scattered across his desk. "I want to find a resolution to this matter sooner, not later."

"I would like nothing better than that myself."

The normally soft-spoken Wade was slipping into the background as the serious Wade moved to the fore. "So tell me again why all of our research is of no value to me?"

"Right now our research has no value because it's as if these people ceased to exist after the accident." He paused. "There are no records following their release from the hospital."

Wade tried to keep his frustration from getting the best of him, but there was a noticeable edge to his voice. "So you are telling me that the people belonging to these names on the documents no longer seem to exist, and it will be impossible to find Lexie."

"That is exactly what I am telling you. It's as if they simply vanished into thin air."

Wade listened patiently for a few moments longer and couldn't believe what he was hearing. "You do remember the reason that I am trying to locate Lexie is to put my wife's mind at ease, not make her a nervous wreck?"

"I want what you want, but this seems to be the only logical answer."

Wade spoke in a terse whisper. "If what you are telling me has even the remotest chance of being true, and the alleged accident that put the girl in the hospital was a failed attempt to eliminate the father as a witness against his former employer, how would this knowledge put Gail's mind at ease?"

The two men discussed the scenario for several more minutes as the man on the other end shared the evidence he had compiled to validate his theory. "I checked the archives of the local paper about the accident and found that the family name was mentioned in the original article and then wasn't ever mentioned again."

"So they just vanished without a trace?" Wade asked.

"So it would seem. The records show that the parents were discharged from their hospital weeks before the little girl was discharged from hers. The discharge papers are the last record we can find of them."

"People don't just vanish," he said. "Do you really think they were placed in the witness protection program?"

"That is the only explanation of many that makes any sense to me." The investigator paused for a moment before continuing. "If we ignore the witness protection idea, the parents might have been afraid for their lives and simply run away, without Lexie."

"I can't see a mother leaving her child."

"Unless it was the only way to keep Lexie safe," Wade's friend said.

Wade was becoming more frustrated. "I guess. So what is another option?"

There was a brief silence. "The option I don't want to think about would be the one where a second attempt was made on the parents' lives, and it was successful."

Wade took a deep breath and released the air in a slow, controlled manner as his imagination visited places he had never considered before this conversation. His mind was full of what-ifs, just like Gail was prone to at times. "What if …?" he started to ask, but he didn't want to go any further.

His friend brought him out of the mental tangent. "I don't want to be the bearer of bad news, but you need to accept that we may never find Lexie." Before Wade could respond, the friend continued. "In fact, I'm so certain of this that I'm willing to wager my restored Porsche that we will never, ever find her."

Wade knew that the Porsche was a prized possession and that the mere mention of it was intended to add emphasis to just how hopeless his friend thought their quest had become. For Gail's sake, he didn't want to lose hope and concede defeat. "When Lexie is found, I have a place in my garage for the Porsche. I will let you come visit it from time to time if you promise not to drool or cry on the paint when you see it."

The two shared a brief moment of levity as Wade thanked him for his efforts and honesty before they ended the conversation.

Wade was silent as he thought about what he had just heard. It made him feel sick to think that someone might have wanted to hurt the girl's family. Once again, the annoying what-ifs caught up to him, and he couldn't banish the thought: what if there had been another attempt on the family, and it was successful?

There was heaviness in his heart at the prospect of disappointing Gail when he did finally share the information, but for now he was going to keep the hope alive. Wade gathered all the papers from his desk and placed them in his personal file cabinet. He decided to file this latest information in the ever-increasing "better not to tell Gail" file until he was certain.

Wade closed and locked the filing cabinet. He sat in silence and thought about the other issues that caused Gail to worry and be depressed. Gail needed relief from these thoughts, and he was going to find it for her. He knew that making this phone call was a hopeless effort, but still he had to try for Gail's sake.

The phone rang several times before he was greeted. "Thank you for calling the law office of Crappo, Crappo, and Milne. How may I direct your call?"

"I wish to speak with Jack Crappo please."

"And who shall I say is calling?"

"My name is Wade Rollins."

"Just one moment, sir, while I see if Mr. Crappo is available to take your call."

The time on hold listening to the recorded message was just long enough for Wade to gain an appreciation for elevator music, and he detested elevator music. Each time the message repeated itself, Wade began to replace the company name with the various ways Gail and her mother would refer to their least favorite people. The message began again. "Thank you for calling the law offices of Crappo, Crappo, and Milne, where we respect and defend your rights …"

Wade spoke along with the message. "Thank you for calling the law offices of Shyster, Shyster, and Doofus, where we—"

Wade's version of the message was cut short. "Hey, Wade. What's up?"

"Just called to see how your fantasy teams are doing."

"More like you called to gloat about how well your teams are doing. Mine would be right up there with yours if half my team wasn't out with injuries."

"Perhaps, but I still think you would be losing even if they were healthy."

They spoke a few more minutes about their teams. "So what's up? I know you didn't call to talk about sports."

Wade was sure that Jack knew the answer before he'd even asked the question. "I called to see if there was any change in your father's position." Wade waited for the usual answer, not really expecting it to be any different from other times.

"You know that if it were possible to share that information with you, I would do it. I would have done it years ago, but it's not my call."

Wade was careful to remember that Jack was his friend and not the source of Gail's frustration. "I know that this is a difficult situation, but how much longer is your father going to make Gail suffer like this?"

"I don't know, but every time I mention the subject, he becomes really annoyed with me."

The silence that followed was similar to when they spoke in person, and Wade could imagine Jack's facial expressions too. He felt bad that Jack was in the middle and swallowed hard past the lump in his throat. "Jack, I feel that it is as hard for you as it is for me to know how much Gail is hurting. I can only hope that your father will one day find it in his heart to help put her mind at rest."

Wade was disappointed but not surprised by the outcome as he placed the phone on the cradle and neatly arranged his desk. He knew that Jack would help if he could, and he also knew that it was only a matter of time before health issues would bring the retirement of Jack's father; the only question was when. A strained smile came to his face as he conceded that there were so many other less flattering ways for Gail and her mother to refer to the law firm of Crappo, Crappo, and Milne than "Shyster, Shyster, and Doofus." He reached for a file and turned his attention to another matter that had his wife concerned.

* * * * *

Back in the living room, the festive ornaments and pictures that had graced the family room were being stored in the cases and replaced by the usual decor. The cabinet with Gail's collection of nativities was next on her list since the dog family was under Amber's constant watchful eye.

Watching how sad Amber was with the puppies made Gail regret having put them on display, especially with how hopeful Amber was that the puppy would be returned. Gail looked at the puppies and had to concede that having them on display was a constant reminder of her own pain, and maybe that was why she wanted them to be put away.

Gail placed the storage box to the side and stood up. "Amber, we deserve a treat for all the work we have done today. Let's go have some cookies and milk."

Amber placed the puppies on the table and took Gail's hand. "Can I have a tart?"

"You may have whatever you like, just not too many."

Jason stopped at the kitchen door and licked his lips when he saw the tray of baking in front of Amber. He had just taken a small step toward the table with his hand extended when the doorbell rang. He stood motionless before turning toward the front door. "I'll get it."

Moments later, he returned. "Vicki and Alexis stopped by on their way to the mall, to see if I wanted to join them." Jason reached for the tray of baking. "I invited them to join us for milk and cookies before we go."

Amber glared at her brother and grabbed the tray to prevent Jason from taking it. "You can sit here beside me, Alexis."

Alexis took a seat next to Amber and was offered a tart before Amber let Jason near the tray.

Gail brought more glasses to the table and filled each one with milk. "So have you and Vicki known each other long?"

"We have been in the same dance class for years," said Alexis, "but I never really got to know her until she started dating my brother."

Amber swallowed her mouthful of milk. "Does he like Vicki enough to greet her with a hug and kiss like Jason does?"

Alexis smiled. "No one ever accused my brother of being smart. He broke up with Vicki for a cheerleader."

"Did Vicki like your brother enough to greet him with a hug and kiss?"

Alexis leaned close to Amber and whispered loud enough for all to hear, "No, but she likes Jason that much."

The blush on Vicki's face was more noticeable than the one on Jason's face, but his was getting brighter. Laughter was shared by all except Amber, whose gaze was fixated on the side of Alexis's face.

Amber pointed at Alexis's cheek. "What happened to your face?"

The room became silent. Alexis pulled the hair back to let Amber see the scar. "When I was a little girl, I was in a car accident. The scars are from my injuries because I wasn't in a car seat." She let Amber touch the scars. "Do you ride in your car seat?"

"Yes. Mommy says that the car won't start if my buckle isn't done up."

"I wish my Mom's car would have been like that."

Vicki finished her glass of milk and said, "Thank you for the milk and cookies. Our friends are going to wonder what happened to us, so we need to go."

"You're very welcome," Gail said, as she turned to look at Jason. "Behave yourself and don't be too late coming home."

"Don't worry Mrs. Rollins," Vicki said as the trio headed for the front door, "We will have him home at a good time."

Moments later, the doorbell rang. Gail opened the door, and in front of her stood Mrs. Tennant. The first thought to cross Gail's mind was that she would need to thank Jason later. She was so glad that she was dressed appropriately for the occasion. "Hello, Mrs. Tennant. What a pleasant surprise. Please come in." Gail wondered what she was up to. She showed Mrs. Tennant to the living room and was about to ask the nature of her visit when the doorbell rang again.

When she opened the door, she was surprised to see the pastor. Gail felt her chest tighten, and she had difficulty swallowing. Both Mrs. Tennant and the pastor were in her home, and both wanted to see her. They didn't mention Wade at all, and Gail felt that this couldn't be good. "Would you like me to get Wade?" Gail asked, hoping they had simply forgotten to ask for him.

The pastor smiled. "Please sit down and join us."

If the smile was meant to put her at ease, it wasn't working. Gail wanted to run, but she obliged and took a seat.

"Mrs. Tennant and I have a special project that we would like you to do for us."

Gail tried to imagine what the project might be. Christmas was over, so there was no need to organize a Christmas crafts class, the bake sale was still months away, and the service project for the hospital newborn unit was going well. She was at a loss as to what more they might want her to do.

The pastor continued to smile. "You must be wondering what kind of special project we would like you to do."

Gail tried to look relaxed even though she was concerned. "The thought crossed my mind."

Wade entered the room and shook hands with the pastor and greeted Mrs. Tennant. "To what do we owe the pleasure of your visit?"

The pastor waited until Wade had sat down beside Gail. "I'm glad you're here. I was just about to tell your wife about a special project we would like her to do."

"Is it another bake sale? I love being the designated cookie tester."

The pastor rubbed his belly. "I can see that we are both very supportive in that capacity. Unfortunately, baking isn't a big part of why we are here."

"Whatever it is, I just want you to know that Gail has my full support."

Gail shot a glance at Wade. "So what is this special project?"

"Mrs. Rollins, you have shown on many occasions that you know how to offer service to others. You are always willing to offer your assistance, whether it is the quilting project for the hospital or your husband's favorite, the bake sale."

Gail almost felt embarrassed by all of the accolades. "I do what I can to help."

"I know you do, and for that I thank you." He smiled again, and Gail wanted to run. His smile was not calming. "We want our ladies' group to learn about service from one who gives service as easily and naturally as breathing."

Breathing easily wasn't happening right then, and the longer it took for the pastor to make his point, the more difficult it became for Gail to breathe. "So what is it you would like me to do?"

Mrs. Tennant must have been as tired of the pastor taking his time as Gail was. "We want, the Angels of Mercy, to learn about giving service, and we want them to learn from you."

Gail was silent for a moment as she thought about what had been said. "You want me to teach a class on giving service?"

"Yes," said the pastor, "but first we want you to give service to someone who would benefit from the support and understanding that you have to offer. Then we want you to report on that service to the ladies' group."

Mrs. Tennant said, "Pastor, please stop referring to us as the ladies' group. We wish to be known as the Angels of Mercy."

The pastor acknowledged Mrs. Tennant with a nod. "The Angels of Mercy will be expecting your report in two weeks."

The short timeline shocked Gail. "You want me to offer a service and report in two weeks?"

Wade put his arm around Gail. "Relax. Nothing could be as challenging as your family reunions, and besides, you will be speaking to friends."

Gail swatted Wade and shook her head. "So who is this person that I am to give service to?"

"I don't know," the pastor said.

Gail stared at him in disbelief. "Let me get this straight. You don't know who the person is, but you're still asking me to give service?"

"That about sums it up."

"What if I say no to your request because I can't think of anyone who can use my support and understanding?"

The pastor's calm, reassuring smile once again made her feel uncomfortable. His soft-spoken manner did nothing to soothe her uncertainty. "One of the problems with the world today is we are too busy to notice opportunities to help. Something as simple as a smile can lift a person's spirits."

Gail still wanted to say no, but it wasn't in her nature. Still, it would be nice to have an idea of who to serve. "I understand the power of the smile. I just want to know who to smile at."

Mrs. Tennant explained, "Part of what I want you to report is how simple it is to find an opportunity to serve. The ladies in our group need to learn just how easy it is to serve when you take the time to put the needs of others, possibly even total strangers, ahead of your own." She stopped for a moment and then with the warmth of a loving grandmother comforting her grandchildren continued. "Call it a hunch, but I feel that you are aware of someone who can use your help."

Gail drew a blank. "Not that I can think of." She hoped that this might convince them that they had made a mistake by asking her.

The pastor was relentless with his smile. "I have faith in you."

"So do I." said Mrs. Tennant. "The Angels of Mercy and I look forward to your report on this wonderful service."

The pastor waited for Gail to agree to do the project.

Gail licked her lips as she tried to think of an excuse to say no. She couldn't think of one so she nodded her head. "I'll do it."

"Thank you. We just want you to know that you will not be alone. Mrs. Tennant and the Angels of Mercy are willing to assist in any way they can."

Chapter Thirteen

GAIL WAS FEELING VERY uneasy. She could think of no one who needed the kind of service the pastor had spoken about. At her worst moments, Gail would move around like a condemned person and mutter, "Then I have to talk about the experience."

Gail was near tears when she confided in Wade. "I have no idea who needs my service. I'm going to tell the pastor I can't do it."

When Wade took her in his arms, she felt that all was right with the world. He held her close and spoke softly. "You can do this! Right now I hear the fear speaking." Wade continued to hold her close. "The pastor wouldn't have asked you to do this if he didn't think that you could do it."

Gail enjoyed being in Wade's arms. She knew he was right, but it didn't make her feel any better. "But why did he have to ask me?"

"Why shouldn't he ask you?"

Gail pulled back to look Wade squarely in the eyes. "That's not fair. I asked you first!"

Wade gave a reassuring smile as he pulled her close. "Think real hard about people you know. Maybe you just haven't considered that you could make a difference."

"What do you mean by that?"

Wade sat Gail on the couch and then sat next to her. "You are always looking for ways to serve your family, whether you realize it or not. When your family members weren't getting along, it caused you pain, and you prayed that your family would learn to love one another again. You felt compelled to have the family reunion because it might be an answer to your prayers. So you planned a family reunion."

Gail sat silently as she listened to Wade and played the events of the past weeks over in her mind. She couldn't deny that she had planned the reunion because she had felt driven to act; she also couldn't deny her desire to have her family become closer. She turned her attention back to Wade.

"You were willing to serve your family to bring them closer," Wade said as he rubbed the back of her hands and watched the tears form.

Behind the tears Gail was experiencing an awakening, an awakening to how shallow and superficial some of her service might be considered. She was beginning to sense that her service could be so much more meaningful. Now she was excited and looking forward to finding and serving this yet-to-be-determined individual.

Gail lowered her head a few moments and then looked at Wade with a change in her countenance that appeared to encompass her very being. "I have been very selfish for not wanting to find this person to serve."

Wade said softly, "Everything happens for a reason, and sometimes we are oblivious to the little things that will help us help others."

"I've been thinking that very thing." Gail gave a soft laugh. "I wonder if the spoiled seafood dishes had a purpose."

Wade rubbed Gail's hands. "Of course they did. We now know not to serve seafood to your family."

Gail's actions were purposeful as she cleaned and thought about whom she was going to serve. When she found Dale's coat draped over the back of a chair, she immediately thought of Amanda. Gail gave a small fist pump and wondered why she hadn't thought of Amanda sooner.

Gail started to rehearse the things that she wanted to say when she called Amanda later that evening. As the evening wore on, she began watching the clock as she waited for the time to send the kids to bed. Never before had she looked forward to doing a church assignment with so much anticipation.

The grandfather clock began to chime, and Gail looked to her daughter. "Amber, it's time for bed."

Amber put up a fuss but finally got ready for bed. When Gail arrived to tuck her in, she found Amber kneeling beside her bed. "Heavenly Father, please help us find the missing puppy before Mommy puts the puppies away until next Christmas." Amber finished her prayer and said amen. She gave her mother a big hug and kiss before she climbed into bed.

Gail tucked Amber in. "Keep the faith, princess."

Jason was busy with his father and Dale, so Gail slipped away and dialed Amanda's number. As the phone rang, she rehearsed what she was going to say.

"Hello. Amanda speaking."

"Hi, Amanda. This is Gail Rollins. How are things on your side of the world?"

"Fine," answered Amanda softly. "You do know that Dale isn't here right now."

Gail laughed. "Of course I do. He is in the kitchen looking for another snack. Some girl is going to find a lot more of him to love than there was before Christmas … and I hope that girl is you."

"Thank you for the vote of confidence." There was an audible click. "Excuse me while I take this call."

Gail waited patiently, continuing to rehearse what she was going to say.

"I'm back. Sorry it took so long."

"That's okay. That's a chance I take by calling you at work."

"Thank you for being so understanding. So to what do I owe the pleasure of your call?"

All of the rehearsed lines disappeared, and Gail felt a sense of panic. "First of all, I wanted to tell you that the reunion went fine, and Dale should be in a good mood when he returns."

"I'm glad it worked out so well."

The panic left, and Gail began to speak with Amanda like she usually did. There was some small talk and catching up, but eventually, Gail got down to business. "I got to meet my birth mother."

Amanda didn't hide her feelings about Gail's good fortune. "You did? I am so happy for you. How was it? Do tell."

At first Gail didn't know where to begin, but decided to start just before they met. "We arrived at the food court and I was afraid we would never find them. That is until I thought that I was looking in a mirror." Gail paused. "I look just like my birth mother."

"She looks just like you?"

"Yes, except she looks older."

Amanda laughed. "I would hope so."

Gail chuckled. "Anyway, we joined them at their table. I was so nervous and excited that I could hardly speak. My birth mother spoke first and introduced herself, her name is Julie Hayes, and her husband's name is Harold. He's a dentist."

"That might come in handy."

"It might, except they live in California."

Amanda spoke softly, "They didn't make a special trip did they?"

Gail laughed. "No, it seems that their oldest son, my brother, moved to a town about an hour from here. They came out for Christmas, and, after a lot of uncertainty, made a phone call to my house."

"So, how many more brothers and sisters did you find?"

"Five. Three brothers and two sisters."

Amanda was silent a few moments, and then asked, "Did she tell you why she gave you up for adoption?"

Gail bit at her lip. "She said, it was for my protection."

"For your protection?"

"Yes, it seems that my biological father had wanted her to have an abortion, and was furious when she told him no. Julie was sent to live with relatives, then, when I was born she put me up for adoption, before he even knew."

"Wow."

"No kidding."

Amanda excused herself to deal with another call. When she returned she asked, "So, when did Harold come into the picture?"

"Julie married Harold about a year after I was born. She said that he was willing to raise me as his own, if I could be found." Gail chuckled. "Knowing what I now know, he never had a chance of finding me."

They talked about everything surrounding the event. Gail told everything she could think of to say, and Amanda asked as many questions as she could think of to fill in the gaps. When Amanda mentioned how much she was looking forward to one day finding and meeting her own birth mother, Gail remembered her talk with Dale. "You know, Amanda, there is always the chance that you may never find your birth mother."

"I know, but I will always hold out hope."

"We hope you do as well." Gail paused. "I just wanted you to know that having people who love me still means more to me than meeting my birth mother."

After they had spoken for longer than Dale would have approved, there was a feeling of joy and understanding that only people in their situation could appreciate. Gail could tell by the tone of their conversation that she had been right to call. Amanda had needed someone to talk to.

"If you ever need someone to talk with, I'm always here for you," Gail said. "I promise."

"Thank you. That is nice to hear. And thank you for your offer to help me find my birth mother."

Gail finished saying good-bye and was glad to have taken the time to offer this service. She had overcome her apprehension, taken that leap of faith, and offered her support and counsel to Amanda. She felt that Amanda was appreciative of her concern. What she didn't know was how Wade would feel about her offer to help search for Amanda's birth mother. Right now it didn't matter.

A pad of paper was waiting for Wade when he joined Gail. "What's this for?" he asked.

"You are going to help me write my feelings about the service I just did." Gail handed him the pen.

Wade pretended to yawn, as he always did when trying to avoid doing something before going to bed.

"Tonight," she said, "while it's still fresh so I don't forget a single detail or feeling."

Wade sat at the ready for the dictation. "So who are you giving service to, and when did it happen?"

"My service is to Amanda, and I did it just now." She saw the smile come to Wade's face and suspected she knew his thoughts. "No, we are not planning how to get Dale to propose. That will be my next service to her."

The following morning, Gail read the notes and felt good about what she had done. She had reached out in a meaningful way. But during the day, Gail couldn't shake the feeling that she hadn't accomplished everything she was supposed to. Gail thought about the conversation with Amanda. She thought of the things that she had said but also what she hadn't said because she hadn't felt that they were that important. Not wanting to forget them, she made notes as a reminder for the next time they talked.

When Wade returned home that evening, Gail had the pad in her hand. He smiled. "It's much too early to be worrying about the presentation to the Angels of Mercy. If you aren't careful, those wrinkles will be permanent."

Gail gave an exaggerated closed-mouth smile as she placed the pad on the table. "I'm not worrying about the presentation."

Wade hung his coat in the closet and winked at her. "Good, because I know that it will be an excellent presentation if you can keep from crying."

"I'm glad you feel that way. All day I have felt that I haven't done enough, and there is something I still need to do."

"Is dinner ready?"

Gail looked at him curiously. "No, it isn't, but what does that have to do with my service project or Amanda?"

"Nothing, but that might be the something you feel you still need to do." Wade put his arm around her shoulder. "We can discuss your service to Amanda while we make dinner."

Frustrated by the feelings that had been her constant companions for the day, Gail picked up her notes and read them again in hopes of finding an answer. She read them several times and still was no closer to understanding her feelings. She offered a silent prayer. *Heavenly Father, I have done what was asked of me, yet I feel as if there is more to do. Is there something I forgot to tell Amanda?* Gail paused, hoping to receive the answer then and there.

Suddenly, Gail heard Jason exclaim, "Nooo!" She finished her prayer abruptly and ran for the stairs.

Gail and Wade reached the bottom of the stairs at the same time, just as Jason came down with a small object.

"What is it? What happened?" Gail looked at the small plastic object.

"It's Vicki's electronic pet, and I broke it." Jason tapped the case several times in an attempt to revive the pet.

Gail found humor in the anguish Jason was showing over the electronic pet. "Are you sure it's broken?"

"Positive. It was making the feed-me sound when I dropped it, and the noise stopped. I broke it, and I'm supposed to return it to Vicki tomorrow morning."

Gail refrained from laughing at the show of emotion. "I'm sure Vicki will understand."

"I can't give it back to her broken. I need to buy another one tonight, and the only stores that have them are in the mall."

This emotional display showed Gail that Jason's feelings for Vicki were even stronger than she had imagined. Her son was being a fool for love, and she thought it was cute. "Relax. I was going to do some shopping tomorrow, but I can do it tonight. Hand me the toy so I can match it."

"I'll come with you, just to be sure you get the right one." Jason placed the toy in his pocket and headed for his coat.

Gail stopped him. "You stay here and watch your sister. I need to take your father with me."

Jason handed Gail the toy. "Just make sure it is identical in every way."

"I will, son. Don't worry." Gail turned to Wade. "Don't just stand there; we have a rescue mission to perform."

Gail always enjoyed shopping with Wade, not only because she enjoyed his company, but also because it was nice to have him along to carry packages. He could be the perfect shopping partner if he would just stop asking whether they really needed every item she purchased.

The last purchase to be made was the electronic pet. They had to try three different stores before they found the perfect match. Gail was amused when the sales clerk went into such detail to explain the proper care of the pet. She smiled and listened politely until the clerk was finished.

Gail paid for the toy. "Taking care of these pets sounds like more work than raising children."

The clerk handed Gail her change. Instead of placing the coins in her purse, Gail closed her hand tightly around them and quickly left the store. Wade took the package and hurried down the mall walkway in an attempt to catch her. He caught up to her where she stopped and stood facing the food court.

"What's up?"

Gail rubbed the coins between her fingers. "Wait here."

"What are you up to?" But Wade was talking to the back of Gail's head as she walked quickly toward the first food outlet.

Gail waited for the girl to acknowledge her. "I'm here to finish paying for the food my brother bought on Christmas Eve."

The girl had a puzzled look. "Excuse me?"

Gail could only imagine what the girl was thinking. "Is the blonde-haired girl who worked Christmas Eve working tonight?"

The girl stepped away from the register. "Just a moment, and I will get the other girl for you."

A few moments later, a different young lady appeared. "May I help you?"

Gail was impressed at how closely she matched Dale's description. She read the name tag and said, "Alex, I am looking for the young lady who was nice enough to pay for part of my brother's meal on Christmas Eve."

"Why?"

"He said that she paid it out of her own pocket, and he asked me to repay her. Is that girl you?"

Alex looked surprised. "I told him that I would cover the shortage, and he didn't need to repay me."

"Well, he not only asked me to repay you. He also asked me to speak with you."

"Speak with me about what?"

Gail handed Alex the money. "Do you have a few minutes to talk right now?"

Alex looked at the other girl and said, "I'm going on my break." She came out from behind the counter, showed Gail to a corner table, and pointed at Wade. "Is that your husband standing over there?"

Gail turned to see Wade with his arms full of packages. "Oops! Yes, it is."

"He looks familiar. I remember seeing him with you when your family was pretending to be window displays."

If Gail had held any doubt that Alex was the girl, it was gone. Gail motioned for Wade to take a seat and then turned to Alex. "Alex is such a pretty name. Is it an abbreviation?"

"Yes, it is short for Alexandria."

"That is pretty. May I ask what your last name is?"

There was a small hesitation. "Timpson. My name is Alex Timpson, but please call me Alex."

"Well, Alex Timpson. Dale wanted me to thank you for being so considerate in his hour of need. He also wanted me to talk with you about something you said when you asked him about all the people in the store windows."

Alex looked embarrassed. "I didn't mean to—"

Gail stopped her. "What he wanted me to talk to you about was your progress in the search for your birth mother. He was concerned about your comments and thought that I could help because I have been there."

Alex checked the time and looked uneasy. "I really should be getting back to work."

Gail placed a hand on Alex's. "Please don't go just yet. I really do want to help you if I can." Gail handed her a piece of paper with her phone number. "If you call, I promise that I will be there for you."

Alex looked at the paper before placing it in her pocket. "It has been nice meeting you, but I do need to get back to work." She then returned to her place behind the counter and politely waved to Gail as she left.

Chapter Fourteen

THE FOLLOWING MORNING, THE feelings of uncertainty that had plagued Gail the previous day were still present but not as strong. She wondered if she had overreacted in wanting to be sure she had done everything possible because she really liked Amanda. In her quiet time the night before, it had been hard not to think about Alex, even though Alex didn't seem too interested in her help. This morning, Gail was surprised that Alex once again was occupying her thoughts. She hadn't realized how big of an impression Alex had made, and she hoped the young woman would contact her.

Morning had come early because of Dale's impending departure. Gail was up to see him off and have a brief visit with him before the limo arrived. "So last night I spoke with the girl from the food court."

"How did it go?" Dale asked as he set his bags beside the door.

"I'm not sure how it went. She wasn't overly talkative, and we visited during her break."

Dale put a hand on each of Gail's shoulders and looked into her eyes. "Are you going to go back?"

"I left her my name and number and told her to call if she wanted to."

Dale's gaze was more intense. "Promise me that you will try again if she doesn't call. She seems to be strong, but I sensed a need."

Gail was still impressed by the caring side of her brother. She felt his concern and wanted him to feel confident that the girl would be contacted again. "If she hasn't called me within a week, Wade and I will dine out every night until we meet her again."

"Thank you for everything," Dale said as the lights from the limo lit up the living room.

"I haven't done anything yet."

"You have done more than you know. Thank you for your kind words to Amanda. It means a lot to her, just knowing that my family cares about her." He turned for the door only to stop and turn around. "Just for the record, I still care more about her than you do."

"Prove it." These were not the parting words Gail had planned, but it was what it was.

Two extra hours of sleep after Dale left were wonderful but still not enough. The constant yawning as her morning proceeded made Gail wonder whether her late-night talks with Wade and early mornings could continue much longer. She was definitely tired by the end of every day, sometimes to the point where she would feel herself dozing off when she stopped moving. But she enjoyed her time alone with Wade, and she felt that talking brought them closer as a couple. Somehow they had to find time earlier in the day.

"Thank you for the electronic pet, Mom. It's perfect," Jason said as he rushed out to spend the day with Vicki.

Gail was about to say, "You're welcome," but she suspected that the closed door didn't care what she said. Amber was content to play with her dolls, so Gail had time to work on her presentation. As she read the notes, she found herself adding more thoughts from her brief time with Alex. Gail reviewed the added notes and could tell that she was concerned about the girl but didn't know whether she was the right person to help her. What she did know was that the feeling of unfinished business would not go away. She hoped that Alex would call. As she continued working on the presentation, the phone rang.

"Hello?"

"Mrs. Rollins, this is Mrs. Tennant."

"Yes, Mrs. Tennant. What can I do for you today?" Gail wished that the call had been a wrong number instead.

"I just called to see when the Angels of Mercy will be able to help with your service project."

Gail tried to politely inform her that there was nothing for the Angels of Mercy to do at this time. She soon realized that Mrs. Tennant was willing to stay on the line until she had a satisfactory answer.

"Mrs. Tennant, once I know of a need for the Angels of Mercy, I will call you immediately."

"Is that a promise?"

"I promise to call you immediately."

The conversation lasted a while longer before Mrs. Tennant was satisfied enough to hang up.

"Seriously, that lady needs to get a life," Gail exclaimed as she picked up her notes.

The phone rang again, and Gail debated whether she should answer in case it was Mrs. Tennant again. Not being one to ignore the phone, she answered. "Hello?"

"Mrs. Rollins, this is Alex Timpson."

Gail was glad that she had answered the phone. "Hi, Alex. It's nice to hear from you." A multitude of questions swirled in Gail's mind. Alex's voice had sounded anxious when she answered, and there was a definite hesitation now. "Is everything all right?"

The deep breaths told Gail that something was amiss. She waited patiently until Alex had calmed down enough to speak.

"My mother was just taken away by ambulance." Alex hesitated again. "I don't know what to do."

Gail wanted to assure her that everything would be all right. But not knowing what the circumstances were, she decided that might not be the thing to say. "Is it serious?"

Alex spoke loudly to be heard above the cries in the background. "I don't know."

"What can I do to help?" Gail was already moving toward the garage door.

"I don't know. My younger sisters are quite worried, and I can't calm them."

Gail placed the notepad on the shelf and got her pen ready. "What is your address and phone number?" Gail wrote quickly and then repeated back to Alex what she had written for confirmation. "Good! I'm on my way."

Gail put on her coat and reached for her keys but encountered only an empty hook. She then checked her coat pockets and was about to check the shelf beside the garage door.

"Where are you going, Mommy?" The sound of Amber's voice brought Gail back to the moment, and she realized that she had almost left her own daughter alone. She silently scolded herself for the oversight. "We are going to go visit someone."

"Who are we going to go visit?"

The shelf did not yield any keys, nor did the dish on the kitchen counter, and Gail was getting concerned. Time was wasting. "Amber, have you seen my keys?"

"Not since you gave them to Uncle Dale yesterday."

"That's right, and he never gave them back. And now he is somewhere over the ocean." Gail went to the den and found Wade's spare set of keys. She was thankful that Wade never locked them in the desk drawer. "Okay, princess. Let's go visit some young girls."

Amber was the first out to the garage, where she abruptly stopped. "Mommy, why is the tire flat?"

Gail looked at the tire and smacked the punching bag. "It's flat because the tire has a hole in it."

"What do we do now?"

Gail opened the trunk and removed the spare tire and the jack. She positioned the jack and told Amber to stand away from the car. Changing a tire was nothing new to Gail because Wade had made sure that she knew how to do it safely. She was frustrated by how much time was being wasted. With the tire changed and the flat tire and tools thrown into the trunk, they were ready to go. She helped Amber into the car and belted her in.

"Mommy, look—your keys are in the ignition, and there is money."

Gail climbed in behind the wheel and reached for the keys. She took the money from the key chain and read the note.

Hey, sis,

Here is money for fuel. The low fuel light came on, but no gas station was open.

You would have refused the money in person, so I left it and the keys in your car.

Hope you never had any bad thoughts of me taking the keys home with me.

If you did, I forgive you.

Love,
Dale

Gail turned the key and watched the fuel gauge. It never moved, and the light stayed on. Gail didn't hesitate, knowing the service station was only a few blocks away. She opened the large garage door and started the car. Gail pulled onto the road and stopped. Her only road to freedom was blocked with emergency vehicles, and visibility was poor in the dense smoke.

"Why are we stopped, Mommy?"

Gail watched the emergency workers secure the area and had a sinking feeling when she thought about Alex and her sisters needing her help. She tried to think of another way out of the neighborhood but gave up hope when the car quit running.

"We are out of gas, and the fire truck is blocking the road."

"Can we ask them to move the truck?"

"No, sweetheart, we can't." She looked at Amber in the mirror and could tell that more questions were coming, but she wasn't in the mood to answer them.

"What about the girls?"

Gail reached for her cell phone and dialed a number. She felt as if she had failed Alex in an hour of need as she waited for the call to be answered.

"Hello?"

Tears rolled down her face. "Hello, Mrs. Tennant. This is Gail Rollins, and I need the Angels of Mercy."

It sounded as if the phone fell to the floor, but soon Mrs. Tennant was back. "How may we be of service to you?"

"There is a family of girls who need some help. The mother was just taken away by ambulance, and the girls don't know what to do. I was going to go see them myself, but I can't make it. Here is the address." Gail finished giving the particulars and hung up.

Gail waited until her feelings of failure had passed before she dialed another number. "Hello?"

"Alex, this is Gail Rollins. My road is blocked by emergency vehicles, and I can't get past. I have asked some friends to come over and help you." Gail knew that she had to finish the call before her disappointment became too obvious. "Please let me know what else I can do for you. I'm pretty sure there won't be a fire next time you call."

"I will call if we need anything." Sounds of excitement erupted in the background. "I think one of your friends just arrived. We'll talk later. Bye."

"Bye." Gail let the phone slip from her grasp as she reached for a tissue.

"Why are you crying, Mommy?"

"I'm crying because I am sad. I promised the girls that we would be right over to help them, but because of the fire, I can't keep my promise."

"Oh."

"But I am also happy that Mrs. Tennant and her friends are able to help the girls because we can't help them right now." Gail saw the look on Amber's face. If Amber understood what she had just said, Gail knew there would be questions.

Gail sat silently in the car a while longer and was impressed that Amber sat quietly as well. The road was blocked, the car was dead, and the Angels of Mercy were at Alex's house. There was nothing to be gained by just sitting there. The only sensible thing to do was go inside and wait for a phone call.

Gail was glad she had been able to call Mrs. Tennant when she was unable to help Alex in person. She felt good for having made the call, but it didn't change how much she still wanted to be there. Fifty-six minutes had passed when the phone rang.

"Hello?"

"Mary Tennant here. I'm just calling to give you an update on the situation with the girls."

"How did it go?"

Gail listened to the update and was relieved to hear that things had gone well and that the girls were going to be well looked after until the mother returned home. It also sounded as if the family would have the attention of the Angels of Mercy even after the mother returned. Gail was happy with the result but was still sad that she had been unable to help directly.

It was past lunchtime before the emergency vehicles pulled away and traffic was able to move. The smell of burnt wood reminded Gail of camping, so she set about making hot dogs and beans. Jason was the first to return after the road was reopened.

As he entered the kitchen, he asked, "Are you planning on burning our house down as well?"

Gail thought the comment was a bit odd even for Jason. "What do you mean by that?"

"It sounds as if the fire was caused by the barbecue being left too close to the house and unattended after the son had cooked hot dogs."

"You mean like you do at times?"

Jason took a deep breath. "Yes, like I have been known to do at times."

"But it won't happen again, right?" Gail waited until Jason looked at her before she smiled and winked. "Are you ready to eat?"

Jason prepared a hot dog and took a bite. While he was chewing, he started to speak, but the words were lost. Before Jason could try again with an empty mouth, the phone rang.

"Hello?" Gail said.

There was a brief pause before the caller spoke. "Thank you so much."

Gail recognized the voice. "You are very welcome. How are you doing?"

"We are doing fine. Your friends are wonderful and are helping us more than I can ever thank them for."

Tears began to well up in Gail's eyes, and a lump formed in her throat. "I'm glad they could help. How is your mother doing?"

"Better, but the doctors want to keep her for observation."

Gail forced her words past the lump. "I am so happy for you. If there is anything I can do for you, just ask."

There was another pause. "Can I come to your house to see you after I see my mom?"

Gail did not hesitate. "Of course you can." Gail gave directions and hung up the phone. Suddenly, the house didn't seem clean enough, and she began to tidy up.

When Alex arrived, she greeted Gail with a big hug. "Thank you for sending the wonderful ladies to our home."

She then began to cry on Gail's shoulder as pent-up emotions were suddenly released.

Gail rubbed her back and felt tears of her own. "You are very welcome."

When Alex could finally speak, she apologized. "I'm so sorry for crying, but the thought of anything happening to my mother has me concerned. She is my third mother, and I don't want to lose another one."

Gail didn't know what to say. Having two mothers was already unusual, but this girl had three. "What happened to your other mothers?" Gail worried that she was out of line for asking such a personal question, but it was out and couldn't be taken back.

Alex took a few moments to regain her composure. "I never knew my first mother since she was the one who gave me up for adoption, and I probably never will know her. In spite of my best efforts, I have been unable to locate her." Alex swallowed hard and chewed her lip. "My second mother and her husband left one day without me and were never heard from again."

Gail could only imagine the burden this girl had been living with, and it suddenly made her own issues seem insignificant. "I'm so sorry to hear that."

Tears filled Alex's eyes once more. "I was adopted again, and then my father left Mom alone with us kids. I don't want to lose her. I can't lose her." Alex fumbled for a tissue.

Alex's story tugged at Gail's heartstrings. This girl had already been through a lot in her short life, and Gail wondered how she would have managed if that had happened to her. It was obvious that this girl needed someone supportive to talk to. Gail saw Alex's need and began to see how selfish and wrong she had been to think it was Amanda who needed her help.

"Your mother is in the best place for her. The doctors and nurses will take good care of her."

"I hope you are right."

As they talked, Gail was able to empathize and show compassion, which helped Alex relax and open up. It was obvious that she had never really understood why things had happened but still felt that in some way they had been her fault.

Amber entered the room and returned the dog family to the table beside Gail's chair. She gave Gail a stern look.

"Amber, this is Alex, one of the girls we were going to go see earlier today."

Amber leaned against Gail's leg. "How are your sisters?"

"Much better now, thank you."

"I'm glad. My mommy was real sad when her car broke down and the neighbor's house caught on fire so we couldn't come see you."

Alex chuckled. "Maybe one day I can bring my sisters over so you can play with them, if it's okay with your mom."

Amber turned to Gail. "Is it okay if Alex brings her sisters over to play?"

"Yes, dear, I would like that very much."

Amber gave a small fist pump like her father always did. "Yes! When can they come over?"

"We'll see. Now off you go."

"It was nice to meet you, Alex." Amber turned to leave and bumped the table. She stood up one of the dogs that had fallen over and then carefully placed the loose ribbon where the missing puppy should be.

Alex watched Amber's every move quite intently as the child carefully stood and arranged the puppies and then gave a sigh when she held the frayed end of the ribbon.

"It's getting late, and I need to get back to my sisters," Alex said. Without another word, she was out the door.

As Alex drove away, Gail watched from the window and thought that Alex must be distracted, maybe even crying. She almost hit Gail's car and then almost hit another one that pulled out in front of her. Gail worried for her safety, but she knew that there was nothing she could do except say a prayer that she would be protected.

Amber came up to the window and tried to look out. "Why did Alex run away? Did I scare her?"

"No, sweetheart, you didn't scare her. She has a lot on her mind with her mother in the hospital." Gail hoped that the explanation was sufficient because she really didn't know what else to say.

Amber seemed to accept the answer but immediately turned to another question about the dogs. "Why did you put the dogs in the other room?"

How to answer the many questions related to the dogs was becoming more and more difficult because Amber was quick to pick up on any discrepancies in the explanations. Gail knelt down, took Amber in her arms, and gave her a big hug. "I put the puppies in the other room because it makes me sad every time I see them, knowing that you are unhappy because we can't find the puppy."

Amber put her arms around her mother's neck and gave a big kiss. "I love you, Mommy, and if I promise not to be sad with the puppies anymore, can they stay on the table?"

The thoughtfulness of her little angel made Gail proud. "If you won't be sad, the puppies can stay on the table."

Gail returned to her chair and reached for her notepad. Her presentation, once almost finished, was now anything but finished. After today's events and the short visit with Alex, there were more notes to be made, and she began jotting down additional ideas based on her feelings. But more than that, she had found a greater desire to help Alex. This assignment was proving to be a lot more than she had first imagined. Gail was humbled to think that her initial idea to offer service to Amanda might not have been wrong, but it wasn't the best idea.

Gail finished writing a few more notes before placing the pen and paper aside. She thought about what she had written but more about what Alex had said. The sudden departure bothered her because she had no idea what had happened to make Alex leave. Gail had lots on her mind and needed someone to talk to. She bowed her head and offered a silent prayer.

Heavenly Father, please help me know what I should do. I have no idea what happened to make Alex leave in such a hurry and in tears. I pray for the guidance and inspiration to make it right. She paused, hoping for an answer. *Please bless Alex to be strong enough to face the challenges in her life at this time. She is a lovely young girl who has been through so much. Please bless her that she might find her birth mother and perhaps they might become friends.*

Please bless her mothers, Gail continued. She was almost in tears, with emotions that had been her constant companions for years now surfacing. *Please bless the mother who gave Alex up for adoption that she will find comfort with her decision. Bless her with the desire to find her daughter so that she may know what a wonderful young lady Alex is.* Gail stopped to wipe her eyes. *Please help them find each other so that a broken heart may be healed, if not two.* Gail had no sooner said the words than she felt a peace come over her.

Please bless mother number two. Gail paused upon realizing she had no idea what blessing to ask for. *Heavenly Father, I don't know what blessing to request for the second mother because I do not know why she would have abandoned her child, but I pray that Thou will at least bless her with the comfort of knowing that Alex is with a mother and family who love her.*

Tears ran down her face and slowly fell onto her shirt as the heaviness of her own heart became apparent. She was beginning to understand what these people might be going through. *Please bless mother number three that she many recover and return to her children, who love her very much. She must be a wonderful person, and I look forward to getting to know her and her family.* Gail finished her prayer and picked up the notepad.

Gail was looking out the window when Wade returned home. He entered the house and placed his briefcase by the door before joining Gail in the living room. "Is your car too good for the garage?"

Gail knew he was looking for a reaction, and she was in no mood to play. "No, it died right there, and I didn't have the heart to shoot it. The neighbors might have called the police."

"What happened?"

"The correct question is, what didn't happen?"

Wade was cautious. "Okay, what didn't happen?"

Gail turned to look at Wade, her eyes red from countless tears shed on Alex's behalf. "I couldn't make it to Alex's house when she needed me most. The road was blocked with fire trucks because the neighbor's house almost burnt down, and because of Dale, I had to change a flat tire before the car ran out of gas."

Wade wrapped his arms around her as he lovingly kissed her behind the ear. "And here I thought you were worried about your presentation." Wade pick up the notepad and read the additional comments she had written. "The presentation isn't what's bothering you right now, is it?"

Gail shook her head. "This entire day is bothering me. Most people can have a bad hair day, but today I'm having a bad Gail day."

"What makes today a bad Gail day?"

"Today is a bad Gail day because everything I have tried to do has been wrong, even if it looked like it was right." Wade's look told Gail that she had some explaining to do. "Mrs. Tennant called and wouldn't hang up until I promised to call the Angels of Mercy when I needed help."

"I gather that you must have promised to call."

"Yes, I did."

"And did you call her when you needed help?"

"Yes."

"Then what's the problem?"

Gail took a deep breath. "The problem is that when Alex first called needing help, I ignored my promise. I didn't call Mrs. Tennant, because I was going to do it myself."

"So how does that make you a bad person?"

"I didn't keep my promises, not the one to Alex to be there for her and not the one to Mrs. Tennant to call for help."

Wade put his arms around Gail. "But you did keep your promises. Alex called you for help, and you were going to be there for her. Promise kept."

"But I wasn't there for her. I never made it to her."

Wade held her close. "You were there for Alex when you sent the Angels of Mercy to help. You kept your promise to Mrs. Tennant and called when you needed the ladies' help. You didn't need their help until you had car troubles and the road was blocked, but when you needed their help, you called. Promise kept."

Gail felt the tension ease when she realized that Wade was right. She had kept her promises. It was not the way she had envisioned keeping them, but they were kept. "Thank you for being so smart."

Wade kissed her forehead. "The smartest thing I ever did was chase you until you caught me. I love you."

"I love you too."

Wade held Gail a few moments longer. The hug lasted until Amber joined them and asked, "What's for dinner?"

Gail looked at the time. It was well past mealtime, and she hadn't started to prepare anything. "What would you like?"

"I would like pizza."

Wade held out his arms to Amber. "Pizza it is."

Amber jumped into his arms and kissed his cheek.

Jason came down the stairs. "I'm hungry. When do we eat?"

Gail picked up the phone. "I'm ordering pizza. What kind would you like?"

Wade set Amber on the floor. "I need to make some phone calls. Call me when the pizza is here."

When the meal was over, Wade sent Gail and Amber to the family room. "You girls go relax while I clean up."

Gail looked at the boxes and napkins that cluttered the table. "Don't strain yourself."

"I'll try to be careful."

Wade finished cleaning the kitchen and returned to the den. Once the kids were in bed, Gail found herself alone with her notepad and her thoughts. She read her notes and found it difficult to put her feelings on paper. Each time she started to write, her words failed her. The sight of Alex leaving the house in tears kept coming to mind. As Gail sat staring at the blank page, there was a soft knock at the door.

Gail opened the door to find Alex standing in the subdued light.

"I hope you don't mind me stopping by so late."

Gail motioned for Alex to enter. "Not at all. Please come in. I've been worried about you." Once they were seated, Gail waited for Alex to speak.

"I'm sorry for the way I left earlier today."

Gail looked at Alex and saw that she was troubled. "Is there anything I can do to help?"

Tears welled up in Alex's eyes. "You and your friends have already done more for me than you will ever know. People seem to not keep promises they make to me, and for a while I had this feeling that you had let me down."

Gail's feelings of having failed Alex returned, and she was about to speak when Alex raised her hand to stop Gail. "It's all good. I was wrong to feel that way. My mother helped me see that. She told me that sometimes things don't appear the way you think they should. You have done everything you promised to do. I just didn't see it that way at first."

"I'm glad that we were able to help." Gail wondered if she dare ask about the times Alex felt that people hadn't kept their promises.

Alex wiped away some tears. "Before my second mother left me, there was this nice lady who had promised to be there for me when I needed her." Alex was losing the battle for composure. "She promised to be there. When I felt that I really needed this lady, she was nowhere to be found."

Gail could see that Alex still harbored strong feelings. Her heart ached, and she wanted to take Alex in her arms to comfort her. "How sad. I'm so sorry to hear that she let you down. I'm sure she meant well when she made the promise."

"I'm sure she did." Alex took a deep breath. "Since that day when she wasn't there for me, I have despised that lady, and I never wanted to see her again."

"It isn't healthy to hold on to things that cause us pain. We need to learn how to forgive others." Gail heard her own words and realized that these were the words she had heard from Wade many times over the years. Only now she could see the true wisdom of these words by the expression on Alex's face.

Alex reached for a tissue. "Today I realized that sometimes things happen that make it impossible for a promise to be kept how or when we expect it to be." She rolled the tissue in her hands until it became a tight ball and then worked to make it flat again before finally wiping at her tears. "Maybe that nice lady would have come but didn't because she never knew that I needed her."

Gail was at a loss for words. Before she could come up with a reply that might have been appropriate, Alex continued.

"Today, I was helped by many wonderful people who I feel care for me, wonderful people like you." Alex wiped another tear before it fell from her face.

Gail could feel a blush beginning to rise and a lump starting to form in her throat.

Alex saw the family portrait on the wall. "Is Jason your son?"

Gail turned to look at the portrait. "You know Jason?"

"I know of him from what Vicki has said."

"You know Vicki?"

Alex smiled, "And I know Alexis as well. We used to dance together before my mother became a single parent and we could no longer afford my lessons."

Gail looked at Alex. "Are you the same age?"

"No, I'm three years older. I was assigned as their dance mentor, and we became close friends." Alex reached for her wallet and pulled out a picture. "This is a picture of the three of us at our last recital together."

Gail looked at the picture and could see the joy in the girl's faces. "They say a picture is worth a thousand words. As I look at this picture, I don't think that even a thousand words could describe the joy you girls felt."

Alex placed the picture back in her wallet. "I agree. A thousand words will never describe the joy we felt." She returned the wallet to her pocket.

Alex saw the dog family was still on the table beside Gail. "When I was here earlier, Amber seemed concerned about the frayed ribbon."

"Yes, she is hoping that we will find the puppy, so the family will be complete." said Gail as she touched the ribbon.

"How did the puppy go missing?"

Gail took a deep breath. "I gave it away to a little girl a long time ago." She shook her head as the memories returned.

"Why did you give the puppy away?"

Gail shared the story about the puppy, and was surprised to see tears in Alex's eyes.

"You really do care about others. How are you going to make Amber happy about the puppy?"

Gail shifted in her chair. "I'm afraid that the only way to make her happy is to have the puppy back on the end of the ribbon."

Alex asked softly, "Do you think about the girl from the hospital?"

Gail sighed. "The girl has a permanent place in my heart. She is always in my thoughts, and that is why I keep looking for her."

Alex became emotional as she said, "You are a special person to care about others the way you do, especially for you to think about that little girl for all these years." Alex reached into her pocket and produced a small, neatly wrapped package. "This gift is a small token of my appreciation for all that you have done for me."

Gail was hesitant to reach for the package. "I don't need a gift for helping you."

Alex smiled as she placed the package in Gail's hand. "Please, open it."

Slowly and methodically, Gail removed the paper. When she finally opened the lid, Gail moved the layer of tissue paper to reveal the gift. She sat motionless as tears filled her eyes. Gail looked at Alex, who looked back at her with an expression of contentment.

Alex ignored the tears that filled her eyes and swallowed hard. "If a picture is worth a thousand words, how many words is a puppy worth?"

About the Author

R.W. HART IS A novelist, technical writer, and award-winning essayist. He has gained a wealth of life experience through hours of volunteer service at home and abroad. He grew up minutes from the foothills of the majestic Rocky Mountains and has since lived all over the world. This is his first novel.

Printed in the United States
By Bookmasters